"You make me crazy."

Marco's head dipped and his mouth covered hers in a kiss so hot, so fierce that it stole her breath, emptied her lungs, left her head spinning.

Hot tears stung her eyes and, reaching up, Payton clasped his shirt, hanging onto him as her heart felt as if it were being wrenched in two.

No one, but no one kissed like this. No one but Marco made her feel like this, and she wasn't over him yet. Not by a long shot. Maybe not ever.

A cry escaped her as his lips parted hers. She shouldn't—couldn't—let this happen, and yet it was heaven and hell and Payton knew this was how it'd always been with Marco. Her response was pure instinct and it was impossible to control…

Jane Porter grew up on a diet of Mills and Boon® romances, reading late at night under the covers so her mother wouldn't see! She wrote her first book at age eight and spent many of her high school and college years living abroad, immersing herself in other cultures and continuing to read voraciously. Now, Jane has settled down in rugged Seattle, Washington, with her gorgeous husband and two sons. Jane loves to hear from her readers. You can write to her at PO Box 524, Bellevue, WA 98009, USA. Or visit her website at http://www.janeporter.com

Recent titles by the same author:

THE ITALIAN GROOM
CHRISTOS'S PROMISE
THE SHEIKH'S WIFE
IN DANTE'S DEBT
LAZARO'S REVENGE
THE SECRETARY'S SEDUCTION

MARCO'S PRIDE

BY
JANE PORTER

MILLS & BOON®

First published in Great Britain 2003
Harlequin Mills & Boon Limited,
Eton House, 18-24 Paradise Road, Richmond, Surrey TW9 1SR

© Jane Porter 2003

ISBN 0 263 83223 6

Set in Times Roman 10½ on 12½ pt.
01-0403-44100

Printed and bound in Spain
by Litografia Rosés, S.A., Barcelona

PROLOGUE

"I WON'T let her ruin the wedding." Marco
d'Angelo's deep voice rang out in the high ceiling
Milan salon. He rarely raised his voice and the seamstress and models at the far end of the elegant salon
briefly glanced his way before resuming the fitting.

Princess Marilena placed a light hand on Marco's
arm. "She won't ruin the wedding, darling. The ceremony isn't for months."

"Two and a half months." They were getting married less than a week after the Spring show preview-
ing the new collection, and the new collection so far
hadn't come together.

They were running out of time.

"I don't think you should worry yourself yet.
Things always have a way of working out," the princess added evenly.

Marco wasn't so sure. His angular jaw tightened,
and his thick eyebrows lowered, becoming heavy
black slashes above brooding eyes. His gaze narrowed, focused on Marilena's pale hand where it
rested on his coat sleeve, studying the opulent engagement ring he'd given her less than a month ago.

He'd hunted the ring down, a three carat emerald
cut diamond surrounded by sapphires in an eighteenth
century gold setting. The ring had belonged to the
royal Borgiano family for three centuries until

5

Marilena's father, Prince Stefano Borgiano, had been forced to sell it twenty-five years ago.

The aristocratic Borgiano fortunes had fallen even as the d'Angelo's had risen. But right now Marco didn't feel very blessed. He was troubled, deeply troubled, aware that the new collection lacked imagination. Inspiration.

It was, he thought irritably, boring. And that, in the fashion world, was a fate worse than death.

Like his father before him, Marco had never needed an outsider to tell him when something worked or didn't. He knew. He felt it in his gut. And his gut was telling him now that the Spring collection would be a disappointment if he didn't find the spark soon. If he couldn't make magic.

But what was the special something?

He didn't know yet, and he certainly wouldn't find the answers with his ex-wife here. "I don't trust her," he said after a moment, his voice low and rough. "Payton's only ever been interested in herself."

"She said her visit was just for holiday, didn't she?"

Marco glanced up to meet Marilena's steady gaze. She had remarkable eyes, the irises the color of caramels, the rich tawny color contrasting perfectly with her glossy black hair and lush black lashes.

As the head of d'Angelo, Milan's top fashion design house, Marco worked with stunning models every day, and had dressed many of the world's most beautiful women for nearly two decades, but Princess Marilena Borgiano was a class apart.

The hard press of his lips eased. "How can you be

so understanding?'' he asked, reaching into his coat pocket for a cigarette before remembering he'd promised her he'd quit smoking.

Her slim shoulders shrugged in an ultrafeminine, ultra-Italian gesture. ''Because Payton's not a threat.''

Marilena must have caught the arch of his eyebrows as she smiled, her full dark red mouth curving. ''We've known each other a long time, Marco, you and me. We've been through a great deal together. We understand each other and we know what we want. It's different from your first marriage, yes?''

Completely different, he thought, biting down on his back teeth, his temper nearly flaring again. If pressed, he wouldn't even call the brief twenty-one month arrangement a marriage. It was more like a disaster.

No, a nightmare.

Marilena stood on tiptoe and pressed a quick kiss to his mouth. ''Don't look so angry, darling. She won't be here long, and she'll have the girls with her. I know you've wanted a relationship with them—''

''That was a long time ago, before she held them hostage, before she used them against me. Maybe once they were my daughters, but they're not mine anymore. Payton made sure of that.''

Marilena clucked softly. ''That's not true. They're still your children. You adore the girls. I know you've missed them terribly.''

Marco swallowed around the sudden lump in his throat. He had missed them. He'd missed them so much he almost felt sick inside. ''Payton knows I'll sue for custody,'' he said after a long moment. ''She knows if she comes back, she'll find it next to impossible to take them out of the country again.''

Marilena cocked her head. ''So, why is she bringing them here now?''

Good question, Marco thought. A very good question indeed.

CHAPTER ONE

DEATH and taxes. The only two certainties in life.
Death and taxes…

The words went around and around Payton's head
like the unclaimed luggage on the airport baggage
carousel.

With a tired hand, she pushed the tangle of dark
red curls from her forehead. She'd boarded the plane
with her hair pinned up, but after fifteen hours traveling the curls had burst free from the French twist.

A black suitcase came sliding out the luggage chute
and Payton carefully stooped to check the tag without
disturbing the toddler slumped against her shoulder.

Wrong name. Not hers.

As Payton straightened she cradled the back of
Gia's head and glanced down into her sleeping daughter's face. Wet tears still streaked Gia's swollen
cheeks, a testament to the hours Gia had wailed in-
consolably for the small fuzzy blankie lost somewhere between boarding in San Francisco and changing planes in New York's La Guardia airport.

It had not been an easy flight.

It had not been an easy month.

It had not been an easy life.

Payton's lips twisted as she suppressed the rise of
emotion. She couldn't start thinking now. Thinking
would only make everything worse.

She shot Livia a quick glance. "Are you okay, Liv?" she whispered, mustering a smile for Gia's twin.

The three-year-old sat perched on top of an up-ended car seat, her thumb popped in her mouth, her arm clutching her own fuzzy blankie.

Livia nodded solemnly, her dark blue eyes the same shade as Payton's. The girls had inherited Payton's heart-shaped face, small straight nose, and dark blue eyes, but their gorgeous coloring came from their father. Onyx curls, light olive skin, the longest, thickest black fringe of eyelash imaginable.

Just thinking of Marco made Payton's chest squeeze tight. She couldn't believe she was doing this. When she'd left Milan two years ago she'd rashly vowed that nothing short of death would bring her back.

And it had.

Blinking, Payton concentrated on the moving carousel to keep the tears from forming. She wasn't much of a crier anymore but she was exhausted and when she was overly tired tears welled more easily.

The last year had been hard, but nothing like the last month. That had been hell. Four weeks endless fear. Endless worry. Endless soul-searching.

And finally at last the truth came: if she were sick, the girls would need their father.

Gia stirred in her arms, black lashes fluttering open. "I want my blankie," she croaked, voice raspy from hours of crying.

Payton cupped the back of her daughter's head. "I know you do."

Brilliant tears welled in Gia's eyes. "I want it *now!*"

Gia's forlorn cry knotted Payton's heart. She felt like she'd failed Gia. The girls never went anywhere without their blankets. How could Payton lose track of Gia's? It'd never happened before. It was unthinkable. "I know, I know, but we can't get it right now—"

"*Noooo!*"

The wail filled the baggage claim area. Payton kissed Gia's flushed cheek and rocked her. "We'll get it back soon, I promise."

But Gia wasn't comforted and Liv, hearing Gia's distress, began to whimper, too.

Suddenly the baggage carousel shut off.

Payton stared at the now flat belt with a smattering of suitcases still on it. An airline employee began retrieving the remaining luggage, locking them together on a cart.

Her suitcase hadn't made it. The girls' bag had arrived. The two car seats had made it. But not Payton's own bag.

No clean underwear, no nightgown, no comfortable shoes, nothing at all.

A five-month audit from the Internal Revenue Service.

A horrible biopsy.

And now no clean underwear. Unbelievable.

"*Moommmmmy!*" Gia wailed louder.

Livia's eyes filled with tears and she began to cry for Gia. "Get Gia's blankie, Mommy! She needs her blankie."

"I know." Payton crouched down, scooped up both girls in her arms and held them on her lap. "And I'll try. I promise."

"Now!" Gia sobbed, pummeling her fist against Payton's shoulder. "Get it now. Now. Now!"

"She needs blankie," Liv echoed, lower lip trembling.

Gia's wet gaze met her sister's "Blankie misses me!"

Now both girls were sobbing uncontrollably. Payton jiggled both in her arms, hushing them, even as she wondered how in God's name she'd made it this far as a single mom.

It hadn't been easy.

"I miss blankie, too," Payton whispered. "Maybe we can find you a new one. I bet there are some beautiful blankets here and you can pick out the one you like best—"

"Noooooo." Gia sounded stricken and her cries grew louder, rose higher, nearing a feverish pitch.

Suddenly a deep voice boomed, "Gianina Elettra Maria d'Angelo!" The reprimand immediately silenced Gia.

The reprimand chilled Payton, too.

Payton knew that voice. An icy shiver raced down her back. *Marco.*

O God, she didn't want to do this. Didn't want to be here. But she had no choice…

Payton battled her own hysteria and slowly dragged her gaze up the imposing length of her ex-husband, a man she hadn't seen in nearly a year.

His dark eyes, the color of cocoa, met hers and for

a moment she couldn't breathe, the air bottled in her lungs, her heart constricting with anger and pain.

She'd never thought she'd be back, never in a million years. And hadn't she thrown something like that in Marco's face on their last meeting? *Nothing short of death would make me come back to you!*

Her head grew light. Her limbs felt heavy and brittle, as if coated with ice. Tiny black dots danced before her eyes and Payton forced herself to exhale, and then inhale. Exhale. Inhale.

She could do this. She had to do this. It was for the girls.

But looking at the girls—Gia's small face almost white with shock, while huge tears filmed Liv's dark blue eyes and clung to her lush black lashes—Payton felt a stab of utter despair.

They didn't even know him! How could she leave them with him? How could she think this—*he*—was the solution? How could he *be* the solution? She had to be out of her mind.

Or out of options.

Dammit, it wasn't fair. Life wasn't fair. Life had never given her a chance!

"Hello, Marco," she said, trying to sound natural and failing miserably. Seemed like she was failing at everything these days.

"Hello, Payton." He echoed her greeting and he sounded so coolly, casually composed. This was the Marco d'Angelo that faced the media, the Marco of a million magazine and newspaper stories, the Marco photographed a dozen times a week, the Marco that believed his own press.

Her jaw ached and she realized she was smiling hard, smiling a tight fierce white toothy smile as though her life depended on it, and in a way, it did.

No matter what happened to her, the girls would come first now. The girl's future was all that mattered.

She might hate Marco d'Angelo but he was the father of her children.

"I didn't expect to see you here," she answered, forcing more air through her lips, praying she'd find her footing fast. She felt ridiculously disheveled her eyes gritty and dry after the all-night flight.

"You left word that you were arriving in Milan this morning."

She felt rather than saw the narrowing of his eyes, the press of his lips. He was irritated. Which didn't surprise her. She'd always irritated him. He'd been so impatient during their brief painful marriage, so angry.

"I left word so you wouldn't be surprised when I rang you from the hotel—not to arrange a ride."

"You need a ride," he answered simply.

"There are taxis."

"My children are not staying in a hotel."

"I've already made reservations."

"I canceled them." His gaze dropped to wide-eyed Livia who practically quaked on Payton's lap, her small knees pulled to her chest and her inky ringlets intensifying the stunning blueness of her eyes.

Marco's hard jaw tightened. "She's trembling like a mouse."

Payton heard the unspoken criticism in his voice, heard the reproach that was always there.

In his book, Payton had failed as a wife, a woman and a mother many times over. An Italian woman would have never made the choices Payton had made.

But she wasn't Italian and he'd never given her a chance.

Her chest burned. She felt like she'd swallowed fire. "She's…overwhelmed," Payton said even as she hugged Liv closer, letting her more timid twin hide her face from her father's displeasure.

Liv's preschool teacher had nicknamed her Tender Heart, and it'd stuck. Gia was the fighter. Liv was the lover.

"And this one?" Marco demanded, nodding at elf-like Gia who glared up at her father, her small mouth flattened, perfectly mimicking his dark expression.

"Gia lost her blanket and she misses it very much."

"Her blanket," he repeated flatly.

"Yes."

"And she must have it?"

"Yes," Gia answered for herself. Her father was speaking English. She had no problem understanding. "I miss blankie. I want blankie back."

Marco's and Gia's gazes clashed and then held. Gia didn't back down easily and she wasn't going to be intimidated now.

To think she was only three years old! Payton knew already these two were going to really butt heads, as Gia grew older.

Marco looked at her. "They're not too old for blankets?"

''No,'' Gia answered smartly, indignantly. ''They're our lovies. The doctor says we can have a lovie.''

Again Marco's gaze lifted and he stared at Payton rather incredulously. ''You tell them this stuff?''

''No,'' Payton replied. ''Their pediatrician told them. Dr. Crosby explained to the girls that they were too old for pacifiers, but understood that Gia and Liv still needed a lovie. The blankets became the lovie.'' Payton's chin rose. *Things you'd know if you'd been part of their lives,* she wanted to spit at him, but wouldn't, not with the girls here, not when they were already so unsettled.

The girls needed breakfast and a nap. They needed routine. They needed time and attention and lots of love, but Payton said none of these things, biting the inside of her lip so hard that she nearly drew blood.

Wasn't it ironic that at Calvanté Design in San Francisco, she had was known for her warmth, her skill, her compassionate approach in dealing with people and problems, yet the moment she came face-to-face with Marco she felt wildly out of control?

''I'm not crazy about the word, lovie,'' Marco said with a grimace, ''but if she needs her blanket, we'll get the blanket.''

He lifted Gia out of Payton's arms and into his. Gia stiffened, resisting him. She turned her small face away, giving him her fierce profile but she didn't utter a word.

Gia was scared. Gia, who wasn't afraid of anyone, or anything, was afraid of her own father.

Payton's heart squeezed. It was never supposed to turn out like this. It was never supposed to come down to this. If it hadn't been for that lab report she wouldn't be here now, either.

Marco reached into his elegant suit-coat and retrieved his phone. "When did you last have the blanket?"

"Sometime between boarding in San Francisco and changing planes in New York."

Gia turned her head slightly to look at Marco.

"So it's on the first plane," he said.

Payton's shoulders lifted. "Or in La Guardia's terminal." It was difficult changing planes in the middle of the night with two sleepy little girls, a tangle of carry-on bags, and a fistful of boarding passes. Payton could have sworn she'd double-checked the girl's tiny backpacks for the blankets but obviously she'd overlooked Gia's.

Marco punched in a number and rattled off directions in Italian. Payton hadn't spoken Italian in a couple of years but she had no problem following his rapid speech.

He'd called his assistant, the one that handled his travel, and he was telling her to track down the lost blanket. If his assistant couldn't locate it from her desk in Milan, he wanted her on the last flight out that day to try to retrieve it in person.

Marco hung up the phone and put it away. Payton felt reluctant admiration. She didn't always like his tactics but they worked. He usually got what he wanted.

Except he hadn't wanted her, and he'd gotten her anyway.

Payton's faint smile faded. "Thank you," she said,

hating the tangle of emotion inside her chest. She'd told herself she was going to handle this calmly, told herself that she wasn't going to let the past influence this reconciliation but that was easier said than done.

Marco nodded. "Do you have everything?"

Payton remembered her suitcase. "My bag never made it."

He bit back a sigh and his flash of irritation stung her.

He never minded helping the girls but he objected to helping her. The distinction had been made years ago. The girls might be d'Angelo, but she wasn't, and she'd never be.

Payton filled the necessary forms for tracking her lost suitcase, felt Marco's close scrutiny. He still held Gia but Liv clung to Payton's leg, trying to put as much distance between her and that man.

That man. Their father. Payton realized it had all begun. The changes. The choices. The courage.

The limousine ride was quiet. The girls dozed. The tires of the car hummed on the road. Payton noted that Marco kept his distance, sitting as far from her in the back of the car as possible, and for that she was thankful.

As the tall stone house with the late Baroque facade came into view, her stomach tightened. Once she'd been so in awe of the elegant house with the high windows, perfectly painted shutters, curved iron balustrade. But now she felt fear.

Inside the house, Payton settled the girls into the bright, airy nursery, the plaster painted a warm yellow and the low shelves in the room filled with toys and dolls. Then with the girls happily playing, she knew it was time to face Marco.

Marco waited for her in the salon downstairs. His suit jacket disappeared. He wore a thin dark brown sweater that hugged the hard planes of his chest, the expensive leather belt at his waist emphasizing his lean, muscular build. He'd always been athletic. He looked dangerous now.

"You're back," he said tautly, reaching for the espresso a maid had carried in.

His voice sounded cool and hard just like the rest of him and it sliced through Payton's exhaustion, sliced through the jumble of thoughts in her head and brought her the focus she needed.

Payton stiffened slightly, helplessly. "Not by choice."

He laughed low, the sound harsh and grating. "I find that hard to believe."

Thank God she didn't feel anything.

She hadn't been sure if she would. She'd worried about this moment for weeks, anticipating the moment she finally came face-to-face and heard his voice again, saw his face again and the fierce fire in his eyes.

Now the moment had come and her heart didn't lurch and her stomach didn't fall. No racing pulse, no ache of emotion. Nothing.

Absolutely nothing. Thank God.

She couldn't have handed over her babies knowing that they—she and Marco—could have been a perfect family. She couldn't have walked away if there'd been a chance for real happiness.

Now that she was here, now that she stood just a foot from Marco d'Angelo she realized that they'd never been in love. They'd never been really together, despite the vows and the ring and the children. They'd been just an accidental meeting.

She cleared her throat. "I didn't want to argue in front of the girls, but I booked a hotel because I prefer to stay in a hotel—"

"You came all this way to see me but you want a hotel?"

God, she didn't want to fight. She was swaying on her feet. Exhausted out of her mind. A fight was the last thing she could handle now. "I came so the girls could spend time with you—"

"And how do you propose they'll spend time with me if they're sequestered away in a city hotel?"

Payton drew another breath, trying desperately to stay calm. "They'll spend the day with you, of course—"

"I work during the day. In fact, I need to leave to return to the office in just a moment."

"You're going back already?"

"It's only eleven in the morning. It's a work day, Payton."

"But the girls—"

"Are sleeping right now, as they should be. They're exhausted and obviously need the rest." Payton didn't say anything and his shoulders shifted impatiently. "You were the one that insisted on coming now. You didn't ask my opinion, didn't check with my schedule. Don't blame me if I have work to do."

She dug her nails into her palms. "I realize it's short notice. I'm sorry about that. But I was hoping you could take some time off. Really get to know the girls better."

"I'm getting married in a couple of months. I will be taking three weeks honeymoon then. It's impossible to take more time now. But that doesn't mean I won't spend any time with the girls. I'll make sure we have time together."

Yes, just as he'd made sure he visited them often in California.

Payton felt a wave of anger roll through her. He'd always said she'd been selfish with the children that she'd turned them against him, but it wasn't true. He'd never even tried to get to know them. He'd visited them less than a half dozen times in two years. What kind of relationship was that? "Your children are here for the first time in nearly two years—"

"And whose fault is that?" he bristled.

She closed her eyes. She couldn't believe they were arguing already. It was all they'd ever done during their last twelve months together. The fighting had become unbearable. The tension impossible. "We'll see you later this afternoon then."

Marco's thoughts weren't on business when he arrived at the d'Angelo headquarters on Via Borgospesso in the elegant fashion district. He was thinking about the girls, and he made a mental note to follow up with his secretary on Gia's lost blanket.

It was imperative that the blanket be found quickly. Traveling was hard enough on young children without the loss of a favorite possession.

Yet on arriving at the office he was mobbed by a half dozen of his senior staff members, each with a pressing problem. They followed them into his office, talking at once. The men's designer, his creative director, the vice president in charge of textiles and home collection—they were all crowding through the door, shouting over each other.

Marco shut the door, waved them toward the stylish modern couches against the wall. "I gather we have a couple problems," he said dryly.

"A couple?" Jacopo rolled his eyes. He was the brainchild behind d'Angelo's successful men's collection. The House of d'Angelo had catered exclusively to women during Marco's father's time, but since taking over the business ten years ago Marco had entered new markets and Jacopo was the first new designer Marco had brought on board.

"Our number one mill closed their doors this morning," Jacopo continued bitterly. "They've nothing for us. They fulfilled nothing in our order. We won't have a single new textile for the show."

"We didn't contract with anyone else this year." Fabrizio, the creative director, dropped onto the low black leather sofa, and threw an arm behind his head. "We'd decided this was the year we were going to go small. Work with one mill. We screwed ourselves."

That was putting it bluntly, Marco thought, rubbing his temple, but it did seem to fit.

The closing of the mill impacted the women's collection more than menswear. It would cripple womenswear *and* the fledgling home collection. "They can't close their doors without fulfilling our contract. They'd open themselves to a horrendous lawsuit."

No one said anything and Marco glanced at Maria, the director of fragrance. She hadn't spoken yet. "What? I can tell something's bothering you, and I can guarantee it's not the mill."

Maria's dark eyebrows winged higher. "I'd say so." She folded her arms over the leather clipboard. "It's the new ad campaign. They shot the first print ad yesterday."

"And?"

"It's not the ad we agreed on. It's not the new ad campaign that we've planned."

"But is it any good?" The ad was scheduled to run in two dozen fashion publications around the globe.

"No."

There were days Marco wished he hadn't gotten out of bed. Today was one of them. "That bad?"

"You'd hate it."

"Okay. Get the ad agency on the phone. Jacopo, make an appointment with our friends at the mill. Let them know we're coming, along with our legal counsel. Looks like we're going to have a busy day everyone."

It would be busy, he thought, giving his creative team a chance to file out before reaching for his phone. But it wasn't so busy he'd forgotten the twins. Leaning across his desk, he punched in the number for his travel coordinator. "Marco here," he said. "Any success locating my daughter's blanket?"

No luck. That wasn't the answer he wanted to hear, and his travel coordinator's solution irritated him. "I know I could buy her a new blanket, but that's not the point. Gia doesn't love a new blanket. She loves the old one. Make sure you're on the last flight out tonight. I want her favorite blanket."

CHAPTER TWO

HE GOT home far later than he intended and by the time he'd arrived, the house was dark and quiet, only a few lights glowing downstairs.

Marco followed the light to the grand salon where he heard Payton talking in a hushed voice. The doors were slightly ajar and he could see Payton curled on the love seat speaking on her cell phone. She was wearing slim hunter-green slacks, a black turtleneck, and a suede green blazer. She knew color, he thought. That shade of green she was wearing—forest with a hint of moss—set off her fiery hair and accented her pale complexion.

She'd always had a good eye for color and design and that was exactly what she was discussing now. Business. She must be talking to someone at work in San Francisco.

For a moment he felt a strange spark of emotion, part anger, part resentment. He and Payton had had their problems but he only had respect for her talent. She was a natural when it came to design. It was almost as if she could see how fabric would drape in her mind's eye, picture the texture, the color, the cut and with just a few pencil sketches, she'd come up with brilliant ideas.

He'd admired her work. He'd wanted her on his team, producing for him. But once their relationship

25

fell apart, Payton headed back to America and went
to work for an Italian designer there.

Payton's fingers were beginning to cramp from
holding the little cell phone so long. She'd called the
office just to check in but her assistant wouldn't let
her off the phone.

"When are you coming back?" her assistant demanded, already sounding rattled for eleven o'clock
in the morning. "I swear, you're the only one who
knows what's going on."

"Well, somebody else better figure it out soon,"
Payton answered lightly, thinking that if her being
gone two days was a problem for Calvanti Design,
then they were really going to be thrown for a loop
when she announced that she was taking a leave of
absence on her return.

She was just hanging up when she heard the
wooden floor creak. Turning, Payton spotted Marco
standing outside the tall gilded salon doors. "When
did you get home?"

"A few minutes ago." He gestured to the phone.
"I didn't overhear anything I wasn't supposed to
hear, did I?"

"No."

He walked toward her, shedding his coat en route.
"I heard you design for Calvanti under your own label now."

"Yes." Payton warily watched him approach.

He'd been livid when she took the position with
Calvanti on returning to San Francisco two years ago.
Calvanti was a small Italian-American design firm
that had shown stunning poise and creativity for a

small upstart fashion house. Payton had been thrilled at the prospect of having her own label and yet Marco had said they'd only hired her to capitalize on the d'Angelo name.

"You've given up working on menswear then?" he asked, dropping his coat on the back on a chair.

She felt a muscle pull in her jaw. He'd never thought much of her as a designer. Early in their marriage she'd shyly shown him her work and he'd been less than impressed. Actually he'd been far more blunt than that. "I still collaborate on menswear and the sportswear collection, but in the future I'll be focusing more exclusively on my label."

"You've been successful."

"Surprisingly so, yes."

"I guess it doesn't hurt being a d'Angelo after all."

She felt her face grow hot. She couldn't speak for a moment, formulating silent protests, wanting instinctively to defend herself but it would do no good. Marco wouldn't believe she'd kept his name for the girls' sake. All Payton had wanted was to keep Gia and Liv's lives simple. Uncomplicated. As free from tension as possible.

"You'll be meeting Princess Marilena tonight. She'll be here in a half hour. I expect you'll treat her with nothing but kindness and respect."

Payton felt as if he'd tossed a sandbag at her middle. She drew a quick breath, the air nearly knocked out of her. "Of course."

"I ask that you'll keep your distance."

Her cheeks burned. "I understand, Marco. We're speaking English."

"Yes, but you're famous for selective listening. You hear only what you want to hear and I'm telling you now that you can not, will not, come between Marilena and me."

"Good, because I have no desire to come between you and the princess. If anything, I want to ensure the stability of your relationship—"

"Why?"

He could have been a surgeon with his cold precision. She struggled about, searching for the right words. It wasn't easy. "If anything happened to me, the girls would…" her voice faded for a moment. Her mind swept the future, saw only a great blankness and shied away. "They'd go to you."

"I thought you'd always intended they'd go to your mom—" Marco broke off, realizing he'd just erred. Her mother had died in the past year. Payton and her mother had been very close. "I'm sorry. I'd forgotten."

She nodded painfully. "Thank you."

Damn her, Marco thought. She looked so guileless standing there, long hair loose, the soft auburn curls flattering her high cheekbones, softening her firm chin. But he knew her. Knew the tricks in her heart. She was no Botticelli angel. She had a goal when she traveled to Milan four years ago. She wanted an internship with a prominent fashion house and she wanted to snare a prominent man. She'd done both.

And yet…yet she looked so tired, so vulnerable just now and it weighed on him. She'd been raising the twins on her own for two years now, and God knows, that couldn't have been easy.

"I didn't bring the girls to create friction," Payton added after a moment. "I thought it'd be good for them to meet the princess before the wedding. I thought it'd help them adjust."

He looked at her long and hard. Was she telling the truth? Could he possibly trust her?

"Have the girls been in bed long?" he asked, changing the subject, not knowing where to go with any of this. Seeing Payton again wasn't easy. Nothing with Payton had ever been easy. "I wanted to get back earlier but I had a meeting that turned nasty."

"They fell asleep a couple hours ago. They're exhausted. The traveling and the time change."

Payton saw the new lines at Marco's eyes and the tightness at his mouth. Those lines hadn't been there two years ago. He seemed to be feeling so much pressure and she wondered at the stress he was under.

"I was thinking," she said, "that perhaps we— you, Princess Marilena, and I—could have dinner tonight."

He tensed. "Tonight?"

"Yes. The three of us. But you might already have other plans—"

"We do."

She heard the reproach in his voice. He hated things being thrown at him last minute. "It's not a problem. We can do dinner another time. Or lunch, too, if that's better."

The double salon doors suddenly opened and Princess Marilena stood there, a hand on each handle, her tall slender figure elegant in a trim suit, navy silk the color of midnight, that accented her narrow waist and long legs. "Am I interrupting?" she asked, her English flawless, just like the rest of her.

Marco stood up, a warm smile easing his tight features. "Not at all, darling. Come in. We were just talking about you."

Her lips twisted. "No wonder my ears were burning. Tell me, was it good?"

She was crossing the grand salon, her heels tapping against the marble parquet and yet she only had eyes for Marco and he only had eyes for her.

"It's always good," he answered, his voice dropping, husky and intimate as Marilena reached his side.

His arm reached out, circled her waist, hand resting lightly on her hip. "Everything all right?" he whispered, the question clearly meant for Marilena but loud enough for Payton to hear.

Marilena nodded, smiled faintly. "Yes, darling, thank you." Then she turned to Payton who had risen when Marilena entered the room. "You must be Payton."

Payton felt a stab of envy. She shouldn't be jealous. There was no reason to be jealous. She didn't want a life with Marco—she'd had her chance two years ago—yet it felt peculiar seeing Marco so warm with the princess.

Not just warm, she corrected, but close. Comfortable. Payton had never been comfortable like that; she'd always felt nervous, on edge. But that was all in the past. Marco wasn't her husband anymore and she wasn't part of his future.

She forced herself to act, and she held her hand

out. "It's a pleasure to meet you, Princess Marilena. And congratulations, too."

Princess Marilena inclined her head, but didn't take Payton's hand. "Thank you, Payton. We're very much looking forward to the wedding. The ceremony will be at the Duomo," she said, referring to the city's famous Gothic cathedral. "The reception will probably be here."

"I'm sure it'll be beautiful." The words were beginning to stick in Payton's throat and no one else said anything.

The silence grew weighted and Payton realized Marco and Princess Marilena were exchanging curious glances.

Marco straightened. "Payton was suggesting that the three of us have dinner together sometime—"

"A lovely idea," Marilena charmingly agreed, her voice beautifully modulated. "We really should get to know each other."

Marco's heavy eyebrow lifted. "Unfortunately, getting acquainted will have to wait. Payton, you'll forgive us if we sneak out? We have dinner reservations."

As Marco assisted Marilena into the passenger seat of his Ferrari, a car he'd bought himself a month after Payton moved back to America, he found his thoughts returning to his ex-wife.

She was different, he thought. She even looked different. Something had happened. Something had changed. Was she having money trouble? Man trouble? Was it something with the girls?

And just like that he realized he'd just made another tactical error. She shouldn't be here. He shouldn't have allowed her into his house. She was trouble. She'd been trouble from the very get-go.

As he started the car, Marilena reached out to rest her hand on his thigh. "Don't worry so much. Everything will be all right, Marco. Everything will be just fine."

His eyes met hers and he lifted her hand and kissed it. Yet even as he kissed the back of her hand, his thoughts strayed once more to Payton. Payton had a way of getting under his skin, unsettling him. And she was doing a damn good job of it right now.

In an effort to keep her mind off Marco, Payton set to work emptying the girls' knapsacks, sorting out the toys and chunky books from the tangled bits of clothes.

It was odd being back in this house, she thought, folding the tiny lilac and sky-blue cardigans and stacking the delicate sweaters on top of the matching striped cotton leggings.

Although Marco's father had died two years before Payton met Marco, the villa still embodied the great late Franco d'Angelo. Which made it especially painful when Marco moved out and left her and girls behind in his family house.

For the first few months she was alone in the house, she tried to keep up the pretense that she and Marco were fine. She tried to keep it together for the girls, too. But theory and reality are two different things.

In the end, she couldn't do it. After their volatile separation, she couldn't manage to be in the same room with Marco and act casual. She couldn't make polite conversation at one end of the salon while he stood at the other. She couldn't bear to watch him talk, walk, work—couldn't bear it when he touched another woman, even if he was just merely helping her with a coat.

He was so comfortable with everyone, so easy with all. Except with her.

She'd heard that time healed wounds but the pain inside her didn't fade, it just grew worse. Seeing Marco, being near Marco, intensified the loss.

It rubbed her raw, rubbed away her protective reserve, rubbed away everything until she felt as if she were slowly cracking up, falling apart, dangerously close to losing it completely. Just a glimpse of Marco was enough to shatter her all over again. One glimpse of him and it felt as if someone had taken a serrated knife to her heart.

The months of stilted conversation and tense existence took its toll. Payton knew that everyone watched her. Some were curious, and pitied her. Some were puzzled, and blamed her. And for a long time she tried to continue, doing her best to make everything normal for the girls, trying to make everything okay. But on the inside, nothing was okay.

And maybe that's what everyone knew.

She was trying to act normal and it was just an act.

Finally, nine months after he took separate quarters, she moved, leaving the villa, Milan, and Marco behind.

''You're settling in then?''

Payton startled at the sound of Marco's voice. She hadn't heard him approach, and yet she'd left the door open in case the girls woke. ''The girls haven't stirred and I'll be turning in soon.'' She sat down on the edge of the bed near the stack of clothing. ''You're back early.''

''I have a seven o'clock breakfast meeting.''

So he wouldn't have time for the girls in the morning. Payton bit her lip in disappointment.

''These meetings were planned weeks ago, Payton.''

''I didn't say anything.''

''No, but I can see it in your eyes. You think I should be here. You think I should drop everything just because you've arrived.''

She felt his anger. It was tangible, a physical thing, black, heavy, threatening, and she stiffened. ''I don't expect you to drop everything.''

''Good, because I can't. In September we'll be celebrating the fifty-year anniversary of the House of d'Angelo. It's a big deal, not just for me, but for Milan and the industry itself.''

She already knew about the anniversary. It was part of the fashion world buzz and she was as fascinated by Franco d'Angelo as the rest of the world. He'd been a genius. He'd dressed many of the world's most famous and beautiful women. Queens, princesses, wives of presidents, international film stars, mistresses of sheikhs.

''A crew from England is here this week,'' he continued. ''They're making a documentary on my father. I have fittings scheduled all morning and then they're interviewing me in the afternoon.''

''Is there anything I could do?''

"You're no longer with d'Angelo," Marco rebuffed bluntly. "Besides, the girls need you here."

Payton tensed, looked away. Why had she even bothered to offer? He'd never understood that she liked to contribute. Never realized it made her feel good to contribute.

"That came out wrong. I'm sorry." Marco sighed heavily. "I'm tired. It's been a difficult month."

For both of them then. "I understand. The IRS has had a field day with my income tax. I've spent hours poring over my financial statements, making sure all of my expenses are accounted for."

His expression eased. He actually looked sympathetic. "But that's behind you now?"

"Fortunately."

Looking at him, seeing him stand there and smile at her, she felt a rush of bittersweet memory. She'd loved Marco so much.

He'd been her world. Her stars. Her sky. He had taken her ordinary life and made it big, made her feel, made her love.

And then he'd brought it all down on her...the love, the want, the need...he'd let the world crash down, her dreams and heart breaking. He'd let it shatter and he hadn't felt a damn thing. God help her, but it'd been the worst pain, the worst loss imaginable. She'd cried for months, cried in the shower, cried in her pillow, cried in the car on her way to the grocery store.

How to get over someone? How to stop wanting someone? How to stop needing someone?

The only way she'd finally survived the loss was

to kill the love. She'd been forced to take all that need and want and passion and smother it.

No more tenderness.

No more desire.

No more passion. Nothing but anger. Fierce, sharp unrelenting anger. He'd hurt her so badly she'd decided never to forgive him, never to forget him, never have contact again.

Of course it didn't work out like that. The biopsy had forced Payton to confront not just her own mortality, but her pride.

"Fortunately," she repeated softly, swallowing hard and pushing a loose tendril from her forehead. "And I hope I don't have to deal with the tax man again for quite some time."

He snapped his fingers. "I almost forgot. I have someone on a plane to New York trying to track down Gia's blanket."

"Thank you. It'd be a miracle if you find it, but it'd be a welcome miracle."

His mouth tightened. "You don't think I care about them, Payton, but you're wrong. I love them. They've always been important to me."

"Yet you haven't visited very often."

"You were the one that moved to America."

He couldn't reduce all their problems to the move. "It was the only thing I could do."

"That's absurd. I wanted you here. I knew it'd be difficult to see the girls once you were half way round the world and I was right."

"You have business in the United States. You didn't make many attempts to see us." She pressed her nails into her hands, her voice taking on an edge. "I know for a fact you were in the Bay Area a number of times and yet you never came by the house."

His voice sharpened, too. "I tried. Every time I phoned you had an excuse. You were heading out of town, or one of the girls was sick."

"The time we were heading out of town, I was going to attend a funeral." Her mother's funeral. After a five-year battle with cancer her mother had finally lost the fight and Payton had been nearly incoherent with grief. "And children do get sick!"

"I sent gifts," he defended tersely, but Marco knew it was a lame defense. He had stayed away. Not because he wanted to, but because visiting Payton and the girls hurt more than it helped. He felt like hell after each visit. Felt like a failure.

"A stuffed bear isn't quite the same thing as a father."

"Don't you think I know that?" he shouted, furious that she was right and that he'd lost control. God damn it, he hated that Payton could do this to him, hated that she made him feel like an absolute lunatic. "Don't you think I struggle every day with the knowledge that my children are being raised halfway around the world and they view me as nothing more than a stranger?"

She took a step toward him. "You're right. They do think of you as a stranger. And why shouldn't they? You haven't even tried to be part of their lives. And then last month, it was their birthday. I sent you an invitation. Why didn't you come?"

He felt the blood drain from his face. "I couldn't make it."

"So call me. E-mail me. Tell me so your children won't be disappointed!"

"They didn't even notice I wasn't there."

He had no idea, she thought, seething. He had no idea how out of touch he was.

Her chest burned and her eyes felt gritty and she realized she was angry—not just with him, but with fate and life and everything. "Do you know they spent their party watching the door? Do you know they begged me not to cut the cake just in case you arrived late?"

"Payton, stop."

"No, you stop. You stop treating the girls badly because you're angry with me. *They* didn't divorce you. They're not to blame."

His shoulders slumped. "I don't blame them."

"It seems like it."

"Then why are you here?"

She dashed her fists beneath her eyes to keep the tears from falling. "My mother died earlier in the year. If anything should happen to me, the girls would come to you." Her voice broke and she turned away. "It's too late to save our marriage, but it's not too late to make sure the girls have a loving relationship with you."

CHAPTER THREE

THE girls woke early and crawled into bed with Payton. By the time the three of them threw back the covers to hunt for breakfast, Marco had gone. Except for Gia's sassy comment about the "big bad wolf" going to work, the twins appeared oblivious to the fact that they were staying in their father's house and hadn't seen much of him yet.

Midmorning Payton herded the girls outside to get some air. They needed to do some running about to burn off their exuberant three-year-old energy and they raced off now, heading toward the garden they'd discovered yesterday. "Come on, Mommy! Hurry!"

Inside the walled garden the twins chased each other with shrieks of laughter. Shading her eyes, Payton watched Gia chase Liv around and around the walled garden. Gia might be more confident than Liv, and she might play the role of the aggressor, but Liv had speed. Payton suppressed a smile as Liv successfully dodged Gia's tackle yet again.

"Not fair!" Gia cried loudly, frustrated.

But Liv just danced away, trying hard not to grin.

"They're having a good time, aren't they?" Marilena said, appearing at the garden's little wrought iron gate.

Payton turned and mustered a smiled for the princess. "They love this little garden. It's like something out of a storybook."

Marilena's gaze swept the stone walls lined by tall neatly trimmed hedges. "This was once the old palace's herb garden. Marco and I are working to replant the original garden." She looked at Payton. "Do you garden?"

"No. My mother and I lived in an apartment. We didn't have a garden." The princess didn't say anything and Payton hastily added. "But I do sew. That's how I fell in love with fashion design. My mom and I used to make all our own clothes."

"And I bet you were quite good. I'm sure they didn't look homemade."

Payton glanced swiftly at the princess, wondering if she was making a jab at her poor past or not. But Marilena looked serene and Payton knew she had nothing to be ashamed of. Her mother had been a talented seamstress and had taught Payton how to sew at an early age. By the time Payton was fourteen she was poring over fashion magazines, copying popular European styles.

It'd always been her mother's dream for Payton to study with the great designers in Europe. Payton knew they certainly couldn't afford trips abroad and yet she indulged her mother's fantasy. They discussed living in Milan, and Payton interning for one of the great Italian designers like Valentino, Prada, or d'Angelo.

Who would have ever thought such a dream would come true?

"They're happy little girls," Marilena commented, watching Liv and Cia play.

"They love all the sunshine," Payton said. San Francisco was beautiful but the coastal fog and gray clouds meant cooler temperatures than the girls preferred. Gia suddenly scampered up the stone wall and Payton clapped her hands. "Gia, no! That's dangerous. Down, please."

Marilena laughed. "How did she climb so high so fast?"

"Gia can climb anything. I can't take my eyes off the girls for a minute."

"They're certainly beautiful. I was telling Marco how absolutely ravishing I think they are."

"They take after Marco."

Marilena laughed huskily. "I don't know about that. They have quite a bit of you. Their eyes are yours. The sweet shape of their faces, you again." Marilena watched them stoop to examine a yellow winged butterfly that had landed on a rock. "They could have quite a modeling career. Have you talked to any agencies? I'm sure Marco could open doors."

Just hearing the princess mention Marco's name so casually sent flickers of fresh pain through her. Payton drew a deep breath and crossed her arms over her chest. "I don't think the girls are ready for modeling. I think they just need to be little girls."

"As always, Mother knows best. And look, here's Marco now. He's come home to have lunch with us all."

It was early June and lunch was being served in the garden. The housemaids had carried a large

wooden table into the sunshine and covered it with a
fine linen cloth then set the table with large glazed
ceramic plates and sparkling glassware.

The twins nibbled on olives as the adults talked.
Marco opened a bottle of wine, a light red perfect for
the weather and a midday meal. It seemed almost natural, Payton thought, the five of them sitting down to
lunch together. Marilena was really lovely. She and
Marco seemed so calm and easy together. They'd be
good parents for the girls as well.

Payton looked at the girls, her gaze growing fond.
They were dropping spoonfuls of buttery noodles into
their mouth between whispers to each other. They
loved pasta—had grown up on pasta—and she could
tell it was a treat for them to be here, eating outside
in the sun, wearing simple cotton sundresses that left
their shoulders bare.

Her heart folded over just looking at them. She
loved the girls so much it ached inside. Did all mothers feel this way? Did they all dread the day their
babies grew up and would move away?

She felt eyes on her and turning, met Marco's gaze.
His expression was closed, and yet intense. He'd said
virtually nothing to her all lunch, keeping his conversation directed at Marilena and the girls, and yet
now they faced each other across a void as big as the
Atlantic Ocean she'd just flown over.

Her heart seemed to fold once more and she drew
in a small, shallow breath, hating that she felt absolutely confused by collision of past and present.

Being with Marco again made her realize that the
love wasn't dead after all. It was just buried. Deeply.

Buried so far below, packed so tightly down she'd tried to pretend that there'd been nothing there, nothing between them. No sparks, no chemistry, no emotions of any kind.

She'd managed to convince herself after one too many afternoons weeping in the shower that it was all a trick of her imagination, a projection of her loneliness.

He'd never loved her and the truth hurt so much she had to take her heart and break it open, empty the tenderness, the hope, the need and pretend she'd never felt anything. That she'd never wanted anything. That she'd never wanted him.

Tears surged to her eyes and she blinked rapidly, denying them now, just as she had denied everything else these past three years.

It was going to be rough getting through this, making the visit work, accomplishing what she'd set out to do.

Lunch over, Marco stood and said something about spending time with Marilena before returning to work. Payton heard the girls say goodbye to Marilena, their little voices chiming together, as they often did and Marilena leaned forward to kiss the girls once on each cheek before Marco and Marilena walked away from the table, arm in arm.

An hour later, Payton quietly stepped from the girls' bedroom having tucked them in and reassured herself that they were truly resting.

She stood in the doorway and watched them sleep. Their dark curls spread across the pillowcase. They slept facing each other as if they'd whispered themselves to sleep.

They had so much Marco in them. She'd always found it bittersweet that she'd lost Marco and yet she'd been given these daily reminders of him. It wasn't just one thing, but many...the way Gia arched an eyebrow, Liv's tilt to her head, both girls impatience and pride. The girls might look delicate but on the inside they were tough.

Just like Marco.

Marco had fascinated her from the start. She worked at d'Angelo three weeks before she got her first glimpse of him. He was there with a circle of others and yet he seemed different. Distinct.

He might have taken over his father's famous company, but he was a true designer in his own right and his work preoccupied him.

Payton loved watching him sketch. She found excuses to be near the salon when he directed a fitting. She listened to him as he talked, absorbing everything, wanting to know more. Always eager to learn more.

She'd call her mother on the weekends. They were brief calls, so expensive, but she was determined her mother be part of her great adventure.

"Fabric has masculine and feminine qualities," Payton would breathlessly repeat. "The perfectly designed suit is a blend of male and female, structure and softness, power and restraint."

Her mother loved it. And Payton had loved hearing her mother laugh. Had loved knowing she was doing something that made her mother proud.

Mothers and daughters...Payton swallowed around the lump in her throat. Daughters became their mothers.

Daughters replaced their mothers.

Fighting tears, Payton slipped from the girls' room and closed the door gently behind her. Fighting emotion, she headed back to her room only to discover Marco waiting for her.

"Does it usually take so long to put them down?" he asked.

She blinked, willing the tears to quickly dry. "I was just sitting with them a while. Sometimes I forget to slow down. Forget to just be there with them."

His dark eyes searched her face. "You seem different, Payton. You're not the same."

"It's been a long year."

"Working too hard?"

Her mouth twisted. "Doesn't everyone?"

His head inclined. "Probably." Marco glanced down the hall. "Do you think they'll sleep for a while?"

"An hour at least."

"In that case, maybe it's time we sat down and talked. Marilena's gone, the girls are napping. We can have a proper conversation without interruption."

Proper conversation, Payton repeated as she followed Marco downstairs to the smaller salon. She knew what proper conversation meant. Marco was going to do the talking. It was all about control. He was determined to control his environment; he was a master at controlling himself.

Only that one time...that one time he lost control

changed everything. Just one lapse in judgment and his secure, preordained life exploded.

Downstairs Marco didn't sit. He jammed his hands into his trouser pockets as he faced her, black eyebrows flattened, expression tense. "Marilena and I had our first fight today."

It wasn't what she'd expected him to say at all. Payton pressed her hands against her lap and drew herself a little taller.

"It was about you," he continued evenly, no emotion in his voice. "She knows I'm uncomfortable with you here. She knows that I'm feeling angry and she—" he broke off, jaw flexing "—she defended you. Said she liked you. She asked me to be kind to you."

Marco looked away, swallowed, muscles popping in his jawbone near his ear. "I lost my temper with her. I lost my temper because I thought she didn't know you. She didn't know how dangerous you are."

"I'm not a threat," she contradicted quietly. "I'm not here to drive a wedge between you. I've already told you that."

"So why do I fear you'll destroy everything?"

She couldn't look away from his dark smoldering gaze. "I don't know."

He laughed softly, laughed without mirth. "I have a million things on my plate at the moment and I can't focus on any of them. It's the fifty-year anniversary of d'Angelo. I'm getting married in less than two and a half months. I'm working feverishly to prepare for a Spring collection that has no backbone, no life to it. Dammit, Payton, I didn't need this now.

"I love Marilena," he continued. "I can't allow you to come between us. I don't know what to do with you, I don't know if I need to send you to a hotel or send you home, but I can't have Marilena caught between us."

Payton felt a hint of panic. Marco couldn't send her home, at least, not yet. They still had so much to settle first. "I'll stay out of the way. I'll work harder at being invisible—"

Marco's laugh cut her short. "You, invisible? Payton, you're fire personified. You enter a room and it goes up in flames."

"I'll try harder—"

"But it's not just you," he interrupted again. "That's the thing you don't understand. Payton, I don't know what it is but you change things, you change something in me. I can't ignore you. I…" He swore beneath his breath and shook his head. "I don't know how."

Payton's eyes widened and her heart slammed into her rib cage. She'd thought he was so indifferent. She'd thought he was oblivious to her. "It's just because we were married once," she answered huskily. "It's because we were…involved."

His laugh mocked her. "I've been involved with lots of women before and felt absolutely nothing when they entered the room." His dark gaze slid over her, and heat sparked in his eyes, heat and anger. "But I can't let this happen. I can't let the attraction destroy everything again. And it would destroy Marilena. She deserves so much better."

He was warning her. Warning them both and their eyes met from across the room and held.

A door slammed in the front of the house. ''Marco!'' Marilena's tremulous voice echoed in the entry. ''Marco, are you here?''

Marco and Payton's gaze remained locked for another moment before he abruptly turned away.

Marilena appeared in the salon. ''I was so stupid,'' she choked, rushing to Marco's side. ''I was upset and not paying attention.''

Marco lifted a hand to her temple. ''You're bleeding.''

''It doesn't matter.''

''What happened?''

''I ran a light. Wasn't thinking—I was upset, about us, crying, I think—and went through the light. I didn't even brake.''

''*Santo Cielo! Come sta?*''

''*Bene.* I'm fine, but the car—''

''Doesn't matter.''

''It does. I love that car. You gave it to me.''

''So I'll get you a new one. Stand still. Let me look at you.'' He was lifting her chin, scrutinizing her pale face. ''How did you hurt your head?''

''I bumped it on something. The window, or the steering wheel. But it's nothing.''

''You need to see a doctor. I'm going to take you to the hospital.'' Marco turned and caught sight of Payton.

They stood there a split second, eyes locked, both remembering what had just passed between them and then Marco slipped an arm around the princess and steered her through the front door to his waiting car.

Payton waited for Marco to call. The girls played with their dolls, dressing and undressing the baby dolls with Velcro fasteners in their nightgowns, while Payton stared at the phone.

Waiting, she thought, was always the hard part.

The days used to seem endless when Payton first left Milan for San Francisco.

The first six weeks had been the worst. Time took on a life of its own, time stretching, weighting, consuming her until Payton felt possessed by loss.

She had fixated on the phone. Maybe he'd call. Maybe he'd write. She checked her messages a dozen or more time a day. When he didn't call she ached inside, the pain so bad she thought she'd do anything to escape it.

If days were long, nights were even longer. The tears she hid from the girls during the day fell all night. Hours of silent tears, hours of inexplicable grief. She and Marco hadn't been together that long. She couldn't explain why she felt such desolation.

She'd cry so long she'd soak her pillow and then when she couldn't bear it any longer, she'd go to her desk and try to put it in a letter and yet all that came out, all that filled the page were the words

I miss I miss I miss

I love I love I love

You—

Payton jumped at the sound of the front door opening.

The girls squealed and ran out to see who'd arrived. Marco.

"How is she?" Payton asked, joining the girls in the hall. Gia was practically dancing around Marco while Liv stood on one foot and stared anxiously up at him.

"Resting. She hit her head on the steering column. The doctors want her to spend the night at the hospital for observation."

"Concussion?"

"Mmmm." He ruffled his hair. "I imagine they'll release her in the morning but I've promised her I'd go back later. It's no fun being in the hospital. She doesn't really have family around anymore."

"I understand." And she did. Payton had no one left, either.

Marco glanced at his watch. "I'm going to take a quick shower and change before dinner. The four of us can eat as family and then I'll return to Marilena."

Dinner was almost absurdly normal, Payton thought, prompting Gia for the fifth time to please sit down and eat her dinner. Liv wasn't as wriggly, but she needed direction, too.

"A couple more bites, Liv," Payton encouraged. "You don't want to wake up in the middle of the night with a hungry tummy."

Marco chatted with the girls, mostly in English, although now and then he switched to Italian and appeared gratified that the girls understood him. When it came to speaking the language, Livia was more fluent than Gia but both girls could carry a simple conversation.

"How have they learned so much?" Marco asked Payton.

"They have an Italian friend. She's been wonderful with the girls." Payton didn't bother to tell him that she'd taught the girls the first two years until she found an Italian professor at the university to come and work with them in the afternoons and every other weekend.

Dessert was just being served when the doorbell rang. One of the housemaids appeared and whispered something softly to Marco. Marco told the maid to invite the guest in.

Moments later a young woman in a black traveling coat appeared. With a smile she reached into her leather bag and triumphantly pulled out a pale blue blanket edged in an even paler satin ribbon.

Gia screamed. Liv jumped up in her chair as Gia went racing toward the blanket.

The guest handed the blue blanket over and Gia hugged it, pressing the fuzzy blanket to her cheek.

Payton glanced at Marco. He was leaning back in his chair, arms folded across his chest, watching Liv and Gia dance. Gia danced because she had her lovie back. Liv danced because her sister was happy.

Payton knew happiness was fleeting, but in this moment of time, everything made sense. "Thank you, Marco," she whispered gratefully.

He'd heard her. He turned and looked at her and after a moment he smiled. "It's my pleasure."

And it was, she thought. It made him happy to bring joy to his children.

But once dinner was over, and Marco prepared to return to the hospital, Payton immediately felt loss. Even after all they'd been through, she still enjoyed Marco's company, still liked the way he made her feel on the inside.

"I must get back to Marilena," he said, heading toward the door. "Do you need anything before I go?"

"No." Then suddenly Payton realized she was denying the truth again. Not need anything? She almost laughed at the irony of it. No, she didn't need anything. She needed *everything*.

CHAPTER FOUR

IT WAS beginning to get complicated, Marco thought early the next morning, as he returned to the exclusive hospital for the third time in less than twenty-four hours.

For the past two years he'd blamed Payton for the failure of their marriage and the demise of the family. He'd told himself she'd destroyed their family; she'd selfishly torn it apart by moving back to California with the girls. But he knew deep down it wasn't all on her. He was just as responsible for the broken relationship as she. Yes, she'd moved back to San Francisco but he had let her.

Now the girls were back and he loved having them in the house again. But Payton was another matter. He knew she had to be under his roof—but under his skin?

She shouldn't still have the power to upset him. She shouldn't have any impact on him whatsoever. But she did.

He still felt such strong emotions around her. He felt intensely. He felt out of control.

Just like always.

The night he rescued Payton from Carlo Verri's clutches he lost his way for a while. He fell hard for Payton and he wasn't even available. At least, his heart wasn't supposed to be available. He and the

Princess Borgiano had a long-standing agreement. They were to marry eventually—everyone knew—and yet when Marco asked the young American red-head with curls spilling halfway down her back to dance, everything changed.

And life had never been quite the same since.

Marco checked Marilena out of the hospital and drove her home. Marilena had a maid to help her with her elegant town house and today Marco gave the maid instructions to keep a close eye on the princess.

Assured that his fiancée was comfortably settled, he returned to the office and was met by the hustle and bustle of the BBC film crew shuffling furniture and setting up lights and microphones.

Marco had thought they were interviewing him in the afternoon but apparently the fashion historian that was scheduled to come that morning never arrived so the journalist asked Marco if he'd mind getting started early.

Actually he didn't mind a bit. It would free up his afternoon and give him a chance to drop in on the perfume advertisement being shot today across town.

He sat down for the interview and the hour passed quickly. He enjoyed talking about his father. He and his father had worked well together and even now his late father's original vision continued to inspire him.

The cameraman stopped filming and literally seconds later two little heads popped around the door, dark curls dancing. "*Ciao,* Papa!" It was Livia who spoke, and she sounded so shy and yet excited. "*Sono io!* It's me, Liv."

Grinning he unfastened the microphone from his

shirt, handed it back to a technician and crossed the room to scoop her up in his arms. "*Si*, I know." He kissed her, and turned to Gia who was giving her father a critical once-over. "*Buongiorno,* Gia."

Gia's hands went to her hips. "*Buongiorno,* Papa. How are you?"

"*Bene.* And how are you?"

Her lips curved a little and yet she was determined not to smile. "*Non male,*" she answered, eyes glinting.

Not bad. Marco checked his smile. She would be a handful one day. Beautiful and high-spirited. Just like her mother. And suddenly he was turning, looking for Payton, wanting to see her.

Payton was there behind the girls, half-hiding in the stairwell. "I'm sorry to interrupt," she said, moving forward and placing a hand on Gia's dark head. "The girls were anxious to see where you worked, and it's a beautiful morning for a walk."

She looked sexy, stylish, dressed in a black mock turtleneck with three-quarter sleeves and an orange and cream striped skirt that reminded him of an American Popsicle. She was wearing black heels—high pumps—and her long curls had been pulled back in a low, smooth ponytail.

"You walked in those shoes?" he asked in disbelief.

She smiled. "Partway. And then we called a cab."

"I should think so." He liked the bold colors and strong graphics on her. The intense colors might overwhelm someone else, but the look suited Payton.

She had the bone structure for it, not to mention the attitude.

"You look Italian," he said, moving forward to kiss Payton on each cheek. She smiled faintly and he saw a dimple flutter near her mouth. She smelled even better than she looked and her cheek had been satin smooth.

"Thank you." Her smile widened, her blue eyes sparking with amusement. "My design. Last Fall's collection."

"Very nice." He liked the flash of dimple yet again, and the wry twist of her lips. He also liked the way he remembered her fragrance, the soft but distinctive scent lingering in his mind. What was the top note? Licorice? Anise? "But did it sell?"

The blue of her eyes deepened. "Couldn't keep it in the stores."

"Horizontal stripes aren't supposed to be flattering."

Payton almost laughed out loud. "It's not a problem if you alternate the width of the stripes." He was teasing her, playing with her and she was surprised by how much she enjoyed it. He used to be so serious with her. That one night at the opera, that first night, he'd been light, engaging, but after that he changed.

"We should go," she said, conscious that everyone in the room was watching them, listening in. In fact, one of the cameramen was filming. "We're keeping you."

"Actually, you're fine. We've just wrapped up here. I was going to head across town in a few minutes to check on an ad."

"An ad?" Gia piped up, interest piqued.

"An advertisement for a magazine," he explained.

"Can we see the ad?" Liv asked, patting him on the chest. "Can we, please?"

"I don't see why not. But it's up to your mother." He turned back to Payton. "Would you like to come along? You're welcome to join me, although I have to warn you, it's a problem shoot. We've had endless headaches on this one."

"What's going on?" Payton knew all about advertising headaches. She'd had her share of ad agonies this year.

"Everything. The tone's wrong. The energy's not there. We've reshot the ad twice. But come with me. You'll see."

Marco's driver delivered them across town, dropping them off in the commercial district with its plethora of warehouses and industrial space. Many of the city photographers and artists had taken up residence in the huge lofts and today's fragrance ad was being shot in one of these.

They took the elevator up and Payton got the girls to sit in a corner and quietly watch the activity. They'd been on enough jobs with Payton to know when to sit still and let Mommy work.

"Take a look at this," Marco said, handing Payton the ad agency's storyboard. "What do you think?"

Payton cocked her head. "It's pretty."

"Come on. You can do better than that."

"It is pretty." Payton hesitated. "And Elegant. Classic. Refined."

"Be honest. You're not going to hurt my feelings.

I know there's problems with it, but my fragrance director—'' he dropped his voice and nodded to the petite woman pacing near by ''—has her own ideas.''

''And this is hers?'' Payton asked, flipping through the pages in the portfolio.

''It's the closest we've come to a compromise.''

Payton's nose wrinkled. ''It is a little flat,'' she said after a moment. ''It doesn't feel…young.''

''I know. So what would you do differently if this were your ad?''

Payton exhaled slowly. Was he serious? ''But it's not my ad. I'm with Calvanti. You're d'Angelo.''

''That's true. But you once worked for me. You know me.''

Never mind that she'd slept with him, gotten pregnant and had his babies.

Payton looked up, met his gaze. He was waiting for her to say something. ''Maybe I do know your standards, but I don't want to interfere. These ads cost a fortune—''

''Which is why I want your opinion.'' His dark eyes scanned her face. ''You're good, Payton. You've got a great eye, an intuitive feel for design.''

Did he just pay her a compliment? She folded her arms across her chest. ''So Calvanti didn't hire me for my name.''

His dark eyes glowed. His lips twitched. He glanced behind him at his daughters and then back at her. ''Not entirely.''

Not good enough. Her eyebrow lifted.

Marco muttered something beneath his breath. ''Okay, they were lucky to get you, and it has nothing to do with the d'Angelo name. You're good. Very, very good. But you would have been great here.''

Was that regret in his voice? Had there perhaps been more opportunity, more possibility here in Milan with Marco than she'd thought? Could it have worked out between them differently?

"What's your target market?'' Payton asked, needing to know since she hadn't read the market report.

"Twenties and thirties.''

"The young adult.'' Payton studied the storyboard again. "The colors are right, and the red dress is beautiful—''

"It's vintage d'Angelo,'' Marco interjected.

"Yes, I know. It's your father's first signature gown.'' Payton looked up at him and grinned a little. "I could tell you everything about your father. I've studied his work for years.''

"So how do we save this ad before I lose fifty thousand dollars?''

"Well, your model looks positively sleepy here.'' She tapped the artist's drawing. "Worse, she's bored. You're not selling perfume to old ladies. You're selling to modern women who want excitement and adventure.''

"What do we change?''

"A little bit of everything. I think you can still use the same set, as well as the vintage d'Angelo gown. The ruby color is perfect, red is timeless and it's always modern, but take the gloves off the model and for heaven's sake, get her off the couch.''

"That's it,'' Marco said, turning and gesturing to Maria, his fragrance director. "Right, we're going to make some changes," he told his team. "Get the stylist, and the art director. Payton will explain what she wants to do."

Payton explained her vision for the ad.

When she finished Maria squinted at the set. "I don't see it," she said shortly. "I don't understand how a girl dancing is going to make this ad work."

"It's my money," Marco said with a shrug. "Let's give it a shot and see."

Payton glanced behind her at the twins, saw that they'd grown irritable and fidgety. "I think the girls are getting tired."

"You're right. We've tried their patience, haven't we?" He pulled out his cell phone. "I'll have Pietra come with the driver and take them home. Pietra's a former preschool teacher that I've hired while you're here. Friends have used her and say she's wonderful. I think you'll like her."

A half hour later Pietra arrived for the girls and she'd brought along a cookie for each and some coloring books. "Want to go draw at home?" she asked. "Your papa has bought you some wonderful crayons and color markers."

The twins were delighted to escape the studio and cheerfully kissed Payton and Marco goodbye.

With the girls gone the studio took on a serious air and the photographer, model and crew got down to work. Payton liked what she saw as the photographer clicked away. The gorgeous model still wore the snug gown d'Angelo gown, dark crimson, tightly fitted, off the shoulder with plunging neckline. But now instead of lolling about, she looked positively playful as she lifted her hands to catch handfuls of scarlet confetti.

No longer restrained, the model's head was tipped back as she laughed in the bright red confetti rain.

"The marriage of old and new," Marco said quietly, nodding his head in approval. "It's the past and the future. She's wearing d'Angelo's signature scarlet gown and yet the confetti is fun."

Payton glanced at him and smiled. "The glamour and elegance of d'Angelo with the boldness of the modern woman."

"Exactly."

Payton could tell from Marco's tone that he couldn't be more pleased and she felt a thrill of satisfaction. It was the first time she worked with him in years and yet it felt so natural.

It felt exactly right.

"*Benissimo,*" Marco said at the end as the photographers took their final shots. "I really like it. I think you've done it."

They left the studio together. Twilight was settling over the city as Marco opened the passenger door of his Ferrari for her. "You must be hungry. We ended up working through lunch."

It wasn't the first time Payton had worked through lunch. "Is this a new car?" she asked, climbing in. Payton had always loved Marco's cars. He took great care of them and the black Ferrari still smelled of expensive leather and the lingering spice of his cologne.

"It's about two years old," he answered, settling into the driver's seat.

"I like it," she complimented, shooting him a quick glance. A shadow of a beard darkened his jaw and a thick lock of hair fell forward on his brow. Her stomach did a flip. She still responded to him, still wanted to touch him.

Marco started the car. "Thanks again for your input. You were brilliant today. You did what I hoped you'd do."

He shifted into drive and in minutes they were merging into traffic, heading back toward center of town. "What do you think of Maria?" he asked after a moment.

Maria had pretty much kept her distance, but Payton knew the fragrance director wasn't happy having Payton intrude. "I think she's still learning," Payton said carefully.

"You mean she's not a risk-taker."

Payton hated to judge one of his staff members. Calvanti was an edgier house. D'Angelo had flair but tended to be more conservative overall. "I don't know. I couldn't get a feel for her. She's probably great."

Marco looked at Payton, eyes narrowed appraisingly. "That means you don't like her. You don't think she's right for the job."

"Okay, I don't know that she's right for fragrance. Fragrance is competitive."

"So where would you put her? Textiles? Home furnishings?"

"Accessories. She likes elegance and classic lines. Your leather collection is definitely classic. Shoes, purses, belts."

The lights of the city were coming on and slowly Milan began to sparkle. Marco took an exit, shifted down heading toward the city's historic center and Marco's town house near the fashion district.

"I don't think I'll tell Maria your suggestion," he

said, smiling wryly as he navigated the narrow streets, still congested with traffic as commuters made their way home. "She thinks accessories are dull."

"Purses make design houses a fortune."

Marco laughed softly. "You're getting smart."

"I've always been smart," she flashed back, still buoyed by the day's success. "I just happen to be wiser now."

"Whatever it is, I like it. It suits you." Marco pulled to the side of the road and parked. "Neither of us had lunch. I'm sure you're starving. Let's grab a quick bite to eat."

At the restaurant Payton excused herself to use the ladies' room and wash up, and Marco watched her walk away. He saw, too, how nearly every head in the restaurant turned to watch her pass.

Payton had a certain magic. She was beautiful, yes, but it wasn't merely her prettiness that caught people's attention. It was her energy. The light in her eyes. The way she seemed to sparkle.

She sparkled tonight.

Payton returned to the table, and he stood up to seat her.

"Have you ever thought about moving back to Milan?" he asked her, signaling to the wine steward to fill their glasses.

"Move back?"

He nodded. "You'd have no problem finding work."

"That's not the issue."

"In fact, I'd be open to discussing having you return to d'Angelo."

"*Marco.*" He looked up and she shook her head. "That's not going to happen."

"I don't want to lose them," he said abruptly, referring to their daughters. "There has to be a better way to do this, Payton. A better way for us to share responsibility."

"You mean custody?"

"Yes. Exactly. I want more than holidays. I want to be their father, not a stranger."

She swallowed with difficulty. This is what she wanted for the children, too. This is why she'd come here with them, but it terrified her, the prospect of spending less time with them. "Maybe the girls can spend the next couple weeks here—"

"And then take them away from me again? No. I can't bear these huge separations. They're not good for the girls. They're not good for me. They're not good for any of us."

"I agree."

"That's why I want you to at least consider moving back here. You speak Italian. You know the city. You know fashion. This is the perfect place for you." He leaned forward on the table. "The girls would be happy. I know it. And so would I."

Her heart jumped a little at the last part. *The girls would be happy, and so would I.*

What did he mean by happy? Did he ever wish they'd stayed together, that they'd tried to work things out? She wished she had the courage to ask him, but it was such a personal question, one that didn't seem appropriate now that he was engaged to another woman.

Yet his words made her wistful, nonetheless. Many times she'd thought life would be simpler if she and Marco had stayed together.

What made relationships work? Why did some

people click and others didn't? What could she have done differently?

A platter of antipasto arrived and the conversation stalled while they ate. But once they finished their pasta and salad, and the waiter had cleared their dishes, Marco returned to the discussion.

"There's no reason we can't raise the girls together," he said, intense, earnest. "We both love them. We both want what is best for them."

Payton pushed her wineglass across the tablecloth. "It'll just get the girls' hopes up," she said after a long moment, her voice husky. "They'll think we might get back together."

"Not if I'm married to Marilena."

"Children don't understand things like that. They understand Mommy, Daddy. Family."

He shifted impatiently. "Then we'll tell them they have two mommies, just like someday they might have two daddies."

Payton flinched. She couldn't imagine ever falling in love with anyone else. Even as impossible as Marco was, she loved him. She'd always loved him, from the very beginning.

"I never even asked," Marco said. "But is there someone else? Has there been someone else?"

Her throat thickened. "No."

"Too busy?"

She struggled to smile. "Something like that."

Marco reached across the table and took her hand. Payton shivered at the unexpected touch. "I don't know how we happened," he said quietly. "I don't understand how we started or how we ended, but I don't hate you, Payton. I'm not your enemy. I never have been."

Payton's heart felt brittle. "You hated me for getting pregnant."

"I didn't hate you. I liked you. A great deal. But there were logistics."

"Ah, logistics. Right." She felt her mouth tremble and she bit into her lower keep to keep her emotions in control. "You and Princess Marilena worked things out and I was in the middle."

He sighed. "We'd been involved for years, Payton."

"I know."

"I owed it to her."

"Of course. You loved her." She swallowed around the lump filling her throat. "And you didn't love me—"

"It's not that simple."

"But you didn't love me. You said you liked me. And it's true. I was convenient and fun. I was a…fling."

He swore beneath his breath. "I hate that word."

"It fits," Payton replied.

"It has ugly connotations."

"And that fits, too, doesn't it?" she said, holding his gaze.

CHAPTER FIVE

HIS dark eyes met hers and held. He looked at her as if he could see all the way through her and this time there was no coldness, no anger, no mockery.

He looked at her as if looking back to the way it had happened, the two of them, as if he could see the black-tie party and Payton trying desperately to avoid the drunken advances of another designer twice her age.

"I had good intentions," he said after a long taut silence, his jawbone almost white, his tension palpable. "I only meant to help you."

She struggled with the clash of the past and present, of the knowledge that in that moment he assisted her he'd changed both their lives forever. "You did help me."

Marco's intense gaze never wavered. "Maybe you were better off—"

"Ravished by your arch rival?" She attempted a laugh. It came out thin, rather stricken.

He nearly smiled. "You made me laugh that night. I was so angry with Carlo, so angry that he'd tried to take advantage of one of my young interns, but then you made me forget my anger. We talked. We danced—" He broke off, shook his head. "We were naive."

His smile faded. A small muscle popped in his jaw.

"We should have known there'd be repercussions. Should have known that even a dance can be dangerous. At least I should have known."

Payton knew Marco had been set to marry the princess, had planned it a long time before that night at the Trussardi's, back before they'd ever talked, danced, kissed.

She'd heard Marco was promised, no official engagement, just a long-standing agreement. She'd heard the rumors and yet that night after the opera it somehow didn't seem to matter. She'd been so infatuated for so long, so enamored that when he asked her to dance, and his arm slid around her and his hand rested on her waist, she felt like the luckiest woman alive.

"I should have known better, too," she said faintly, looking away, feeling painfully exposed. "I'd heard you were promised to the princess, and I don't know if I didn't believe it, or if I didn't care, but I got swept away by the magic that night. First the opera at La Scala, and then the party at the Trussardi palace, and then you."

He was looking at her, his brows pulled, his expression intense.

"I felt like Cinderella at the ball," she said. She'd been a virgin and embarrassingly inexperienced but when Marco started kissing her something happened inside her. There was no stopping, no thinking, no control. She just wanted to feel more. She wanted to feel everything. "I got carried away and I didn't think until it was all over."

His mouth twisted. "Was I that good?"

Payton's face burned hot. Her heart beat wildly. He was better than good. He was brilliant. She sucked in a quick breath, fought to control her emotions. "It was perfect and it was my first time."

Marco paid the dinner bill and they returned to his car and headed home.

They drove through the dark streets in silence and Payton stared out her window at the blur of passing buildings.

He'd said they were naive and he was right. She, especially. She'd never bought into auras and mystical elements but the night she saw him at the La Scala mingling with the glittering crowd during the intermission, everything felt so clear and bright. It was as if fate and the future had come together in a gorgeous glaze of light.

She'd never forget the moment he turned his head and looked at her, directly at her.

He was wearing a tuxedo without a bow tie and his white shirt was open at the throat. His dark hair was rather long, he always wore it long, and brushed the collar of his starched shirt, fell rakishly across the brow.

As he turned his head to look at her, one dark eyebrow arched ever so slightly and there was a glint in his eye. He looked very sexy…and a bit wicked…and when his dark eyes met hers she felt as if she'd glimpsed life itself.

There was time, she thought, and then there was time in Marco d'Angelo's eyes.

She remembered how the bell sounded in the opera

house, signaling the end of intermission and he and his circle of beautiful people moved on. Payton stood transfixed, legs shaking, watching him walk away. But she knew in a strange sixth sense sort of way that they weren't finished yet.

Marco took a tight corner, his black Ferrari hugging the turn and Payton gripped the door handle to keep from falling sideways in her seat. No, they hadn't been finished that night at La Scala. They hadn't even begun yet.

Marco pulled into his parking garage. "About earlier, at the photo shoot," he said, breaking the silence. "Your suggestions were dead-on. I don't know how you do it, but you were wonderful. I couldn't have asked for better. Thank you."

"You're welcome."

He hesitated for a moment and then turned off the ignition. "Marilena is good with children," he said in a flat voice. "She thinks our daughters are precious, and as you might have guessed, we hope to have our own someday."

Payton didn't know why he had to do this now, tonight, after such a wonderful day. "I see."

"Marilena will be a wonderful mother."

"I'm sure she will," Payton answered faintly.

"I know we'll have at least one or two babies, but she assures me that the twins will never play second fiddle. They'll always be important."

If he'd hoped to reassure her, he was failing, Payton thought, glancing at her hands. "Where do you plan to live?"

"Here, of course."

His house. *Their* house. Their former house. Pain suffused her chest, a rush of memory. "Great." She looked up at him, eyes burning and praying he couldn't see the sheen of tears. "Anything else?"

"No."

The girls were still up and Payton read them a story before Marco appeared in the nursery to help tuck them in. Payton stepped back to give Marco room and she watched from the doorway as he said prayers with them and then blessed each and kissed Gia, and then Liv good-night.

Her heart ached as she saw Liv slip her arms around Marco's neck and hold him close for an extra moment. "I love you, Papa," Liv whispered shyly.

"I love you, too," he answered, kissing her. He stood and looked down at his daughters and lightly touched each child's head. *"Buonanotte, bambini."*

It was time to tell him. It was time to tell him the truth. This wasn't going to be easy, but then she didn't think it would ever be.

Payton followed Marco from the girls bedroom. "Would you care for a drink?" he asked, as they reached the head of the stairs.

"Thank you."

They entered his private sitting room, the creamy plaster walls lined in places with pale floor to ceiling bookshelves, although only half the shelves held books. The rest of the shelves were devoted to art— bronzes, miniatures, relics of past civilizations.

"Have you thought any more about coming to work for me? I'm serious, you know," Marco said, calmly pouring her a generous glass of sweet after dinner wine.

"I'll find you a place to live near the fashion district. In fact, I know of a great house coming on the market on Via della Spiga," he said, naming a street just a few blocks from his headquarters. "It has a beautiful courtyard garden, the rooms are large and bright. The house gets excellent light."

His words rushed over her in a river of sound and feeling. "I can't," she said at last. "At least not now."

"Why not?"

"It's complicated, but trust me when I say I can't move here for a while. Six months…a year…at least."

"You're going to take the girls away for another year?"

"No. I won't take them away. I—" She broke off, swallowed, and pressed on, "I thought I'd leave them here."

"Leave them?"

Payton half-closed her eyes, unwilling to go where her emotions were leading her. The girls, she reminded herself, think of the girls. If nothing else, think of their innocence. They don't know that bad things can happen to their mommy and daddy yet.

That bad things *will* happen.

Her eyes felt gritty. They burned and Payton turned as if to go but realized she had nowhere to go. There was no one she could turn to anymore.

There was just Marco.

The stark reality made her head swim. Her legs felt

as if they'd give way any minute and she turned away, fighting the tears, fighting all that she was trying so hard to handle on her own.

"Payton, what is it?"

The intensity in his voice nearly undid her. Part of her longed to tell him everything and yet another part of her was still so afraid. It was that old fear of naming something…of giving something of substance…existence…power.

She couldn't give the disease power. She knew the power it had. She knew what had happened to her mother and aunt.

"Payton, talk to me."

"I don't think I can."

He swiftly moved toward her, his hands circling her upper arms. "Why not? You can talk to everyone else. Why can't you talk to me?"

When she didn't answer, he clasped her chin, lifted her face to his. "You know me, Payton. You know me better than anyone."

"Maybe that's the problem."

His intense expression pierced her, driving holes of hurt into her heart.

"God forgive me, but you make me crazy." He swore softly just before his head dipped and his mouth covered hers in a kiss so hot, so fierce that it stole her breath, emptied her lungs, left her head spinning.

Hot tears stung her eyes and reaching up, Payton clasped his shirt, hanging on to him as her heart felt as if it were being wrenched in two.

No one, but no one kissed like this. No one but

Marco made her feel like this and God in heaven, she wasn't over him yet. Not by a long shot. Maybe not ever.

A cry escaped her as his lips parted hers. She felt wildly divergent emotions—pain, pleasure, denial. What on earth was she doing? The last time he'd kissed her like this it'd been in the gardens of the Trussardi family palazzo. They'd both lost control then and they both knew what had happened since.

There were consequences, her brain shouted, there are always consequences.

She shouldn't—couldn't—let this happen and yet it was heaven and hell and Payton knew this was how it'd always been with Marco. Her response was pure instinct and it was impossible to control.

Her whimper seemed to push him to the edge. Marco's thumb stroked close to the corner of her mouth, lighting fire beneath her skin, making her crave more and she shifted beneath him, the pressure of his mouth parting hers and she felt open and naked as his tongue caressed the inside of her lower lip.

Her hands were knotted in his shirt, her breasts pressed to his hard chest, her body straining and it was still not enough, she thought dimly, body hot, tingling, feverish, this kiss and this limited touch wasn't enough. She arched closer, felt his hand shift from her arm to her hip as he dragged her even closer, and battling a groan she felt him press against her, his body hard, tense, barely controlled.

He'll hate himself later. She heard the warning, knew the warning as the voice of reality. Sanity and gasping for air, she broke free, using her palms to push him away.

His dark eyes glittered, his cheekbones glowed red. "You."

His voice was deep, thick, accent pronounced. She'd wanted the kiss to continue, hadn't wanted to end it but she knew Marco, knew he'd resent the loss of control—no matter how brief.

There would be consequences—no, make that hell to pay.

She was right. He drew another shallow breath.

"Maledizione!" He swore bitterly, battling to control his breathing. "Why do I do this? What is the matter with me?"

"Marco—"

"No. Don't say anything. You'll only make it worse."

Payton's gaze searched the taut planes of his face, his features hard, his mouth pinched.

He took a menacing step toward her, his finger pointed. "I nearly broke her heart once. I nearly crushed her, and she's fragile, Payton, she's not like you. She can't handle the rejection."

"I'm sorry. It won't happen again."

"No, it won't, because I want you to go. I want you to get your things, your luggage, your children and go. *Now.*"

Payton's heart rose. "*My* children?"

"It's what you wanted. It's why you kept them from me."

"Marco." He was angry and he was lashing out at

her, she understood that much, but to be cruel about the children? That just wasn't fair.

"You moved halfway around the world. You turned me into a stranger. This is your doing, Payton!"

She had to stay calm, had to keep control. "I'm trying to make amends—"

"How?" he interrupted fiercely. "By destroying my relationship with Marilena?"

"Nothing's destroyed, Marco. Nothing's changed. Don't blow this out of proportion. It was just a kiss—"

"Just a kiss? How can you say that? I'm *engaged.* I'm about to marry Marilena in two months and you say, you have the gall to say, it's just a kiss?"

He'd paled, blood draining, intensifying the hard slash of cheekbone and broad jaw.

"Maybe a kiss is nothing to you," he continued bitterly, "but I am loyal. I am faithful. I do not do things like this. I do not make love to one woman when promised to another and yet twice now I've done the unthinkable and both times it was with you."

"I'm sorry."

"What is it about you, Payton?"

"I don't know."

"I don't know either, but this…this—" He broke off, lips twisting, filled with loathing and self-disgust. "This is wrong. I am ashamed."

He was. She didn't doubt him, or his sincerity for a moment. "I'll go to my room. I'll give you some space."

"That's not what I asked you to do." He was standing over her, shoulders dwarfing her. "I said get your suitcases and go."

"Marco, please——"

"No! I am done talking. I am sick inside, I am sick that we are back to where we were three years ago. I don't know what you do to me, I don't understand the effect you have on me but this time I know exactly what to do. Get rid of you." Tiny beads of sweat formed on his brow. Tendons popped on his neck. "Fast."

They were standing so close she could feel his warmth, feel rather than see the rise and fall of his chest. He was insisting she, demanding she leave, but she could not.

She would not.

Yet.

He cursed beneath his breath. "If you will not leave, than I shall." He stepped around her as if she were foul. Tainted. "Marilena and I will stay at my country house at the lake until you're gone."

Payton struggled to find her voice as he reached the tall, painted salon doors with the whirl of pale turquoise against faded gold.

Stop him. Stop him. You can't let him leave. "You don't have to go."

He stopped, his wide back filling the doorway, but he didn't turn around nor glance behind.

She drew a shaky breath. "I will go. I'll pack my things immediately." She forced herself to speak, to keep the words coming even though she felt horribly disorganized, her emotions colliding with her reason. "But I shall not be taking the girls back with me."

Ah. She had his attention now. He hadn't turned around, but his head lowered and she caught sight of his profile.

"What nonsense is this?" His low voice throbbed with fury.

"It's not nonsense. It's true. I can't take them home. I won't have them watch me go through chemo."

He said nothing. He hadn't moved. She pushed herself on. "I know what the treatment looks like, Marco. I know how it ravages the body. I don't want the girls exposed to that."

He stood frozen in place. "Chemo?"

His voice came out rough. Payton touched her tongue to her upper lip and took a deep breath. Damn but this was hard. One minute she was kissing, feeling, wanting and the next she was an ice maiden again, frozen on the inside.

"I…" She looked up at him, wondered how she'd get the words out. She hadn't spoken them aloud yet. Hadn't told anyone. "I have cancer."

He turned toward her. She didn't just say what he thought she said, did she?

He did a slow double-take as he faced her and yet Payton didn't look hysterical. She looked calm. Astonishingly calm. She couldn't have said what he thought she'd said. It was crazy, but for a split-second he actually thought she'd said she had cancer.

"Mommy!" The cry sounded outside the study, at the top of the stairs.

Payton quickly opened the door and headed for the stairs.

"I have to go to the bathroom." Gia was standing on the stairs in her nightgown. "I have to go bad but I'm scared."

It took Payton awhile to get Gia settled back into bed and by the time she'd closed the door to the girls' bedroom, Marco was no longer in his study.

She found him outside, leaning against a column in the courtyard. He didn't turn around but he must have heard her. "This is true?" he asked, staring up at the sky.

"Yes."

"You've gone for a second opinion?"

"Yes. I'm waiting on the results, but the first diagnosis came from the specialist who treated my mother." She stepped past him to stand in the middle of the courtyard in a small pool of moonlight. "I'm lucky they picked it up when they did. The earlier it's detected the better my chances."

"You haven't told the girls."

"No." Payton felt a welling of fear. "I love them, Marco. They're everything to me."

His expression didn't change. "So you did have an ulterior motive in coming to see me. It's not just that the girls are older and easier to travel with. And it's not about the girls missing me. It's about you."

She didn't say anything and he swore softly, bitterly and shook his head.

"*Maledizione,*" he cursed beneath his breath. "I should have known better. You'd never come to me on your own. You only came because you were desperate."

CHAPTER SIX

PAYTON swallowed the hurt protest. He was right. She wouldn't have come to see him if she weren't desperate.

Her mother's death had left her without options. With her gone, she had no other living family member left, no one who could help her with the children while she underwent treatment.

So she came here, back to Marco's home and in a painful, bittersweet paradox—it was exactly the right thing to do. Fate and circumstance forced her to do what her pride wouldn't allow her. Fate and circumstance required humility and she had no other choice but to throw herself at Marco's feet.

Beg for help, if not mercy.

"You smile," he said tersely.

"A little." A headache was forming and she pulled the elastic from her hair, letting the long curls fall loose. "But only because you're right. You know how I hate to be wrong, especially if it means you're right."

His hard chiseled face gave away nothing. "Pride."

"Pride's always been a problem for me. Maybe growing up poor caused that. Maybe it's because everyone knew my dad had left my mom—" She broke off, swallowed the sour taste in her mouth.

She was in kindergarten when her father finally left for good. Her parents had been fighting for months and the fighting escalated until everything seemed to be flying in perpetual motion across the living room—books, purses, shoes, car keys, telephones. Then one day the shouting stopped. Nothing was thrown anymore. No one ever slammed a door again. Dad had gone. And everyone knew.

Absolutely everyone.

Payton slowly sank down on a garden seat. "Everyone knew you married me because I'd gotten pregnant." She consciously forced herself to relax, to take a deep breath. *Inhale, exhale, inhale—nothing bad was going to happen.* "I hated it. I hated that people—" she felt his gaze and she looked up at him "—pitied you."

"Pitied *me?*"

She nodded, her neck stiff, her body sore. She felt as if she'd been through the spin cycle on a washing machine. "You were Marco d'Angelo. You could have married anyone, and you'd intended to marry a princess. Instead you got stuck with me."

"So you went home."

She felt her cheeks burn. "Home to hide."

Marco looked at her for a long moment before moving away, walking to the far end of the courtyard toward the house. "Pride," he repeated slowly, softly, as if experimenting with the word. His scrutiny was hard. There was nothing gentle in his expression.

"If there's any irony," she said to fill the strained silence. "It's that I'm at the end of my rope. I've no pride left. Nothing holding me back anymore. I am desperate. I need you. I need your help.''

He stared at her but didn't speak. Yet he didn't need words to communicate. She felt his anger, and his frustration. It was happening all over again. They were back to the awful sense of being trapped... cornered. It was what forced them to marry in the first place and now they were confronted by a reality bigger than either of them once again.

''Please, Marco, please help me make this transition work for them,'' she continued softly, urgently, her hands knotted as if in prayer. ''Help me feel like I've done something right in my life.''

''Of course you've done something right in life,'' he answered sharply, unable to bear all the words, so much sound, when he felt so utterly confused by it all.

How could she have cancer? She was so young! And she didn't look the least bit sick. In fact, he'd never seen her so radiant.

Today at the photo shoot she'd taken his breath away and he'd found himself enchanted with the curve of her cheekbone, line of her jaw, high arching eyebrow. She was like a work of art herself and even if they didn't always agree, and even if they'd had problems between them, he'd never wish her ill. Never, ever.

''I'm sorry, Marco.'' She was looking at him, dark blue eyes worried. They were Livia's eyes, and she was looking to him for reassurance. Forgiveness. It wounded him. Did she think she needed forgiveness—and from him of all people?

They'd had problems, a lot of problems, but there had also been moments of good—not to mention moments of lightness and sweetness that he'd never known with anyone else before. Payton might not be regal and controlled like Marilena but she was warm and funny and passionate about life and that passion was addictive.

She was addictive. He'd responded to her from the beginning and it had happened again tonight—the attraction, the desire, the hunger for someone and something utterly different from himself.

"You have to know I never wanted this to happen," she added huskily. "Never wanted to hurt the girls, or inconvenience you."

The words were endless, he thought, sound and more sound and he'd heard enough. There were words and there was action. There was what one said and what one did.

He was sick of getting nowhere and accomplishing nothing. Endless talk. Wasted time.

Three years of wasted time.

Payton realized she was the only one talking. Marco wasn't saying anything. He was just staring at her, and there was no expression in his eyes or face.

If only he'd say something. *Anything*. "If they're happy, I can be happy," she whispered, her voice was thickening with unshed tears. "If I know they love being with you then I'm okay when I go home and do what I'll have to do."

"When did you intend to go home?"

Marco's question flattened her. She drew a breath,

held it in and then slowly exhaled. "I'm holding a reservation for a week from Tuesday."

"Nine days from now."

"Yes."

"And your treatment would begin when?"

"A week or so after that. There are some details to still be hammered out. More tests, and then hospital scheduling."

Marco moved away, walking toward the other end of the courtyard. Payton watched him pace. He seemed lost in thought and periodically he reached up to rub the back of his neck. "You want the girls to stay here, with me, while you begin treatment?"

"I think it's best."

He stared at a fixed point, his expression shuttered. "They'll be frightened being left behind."

"Perhaps a little, but I think we can ease their fear if we're united on this. If we're friendly and the girls know they're not being abandoned."

He'd begun to pace the room. His chest burned and his head throbbed and the last four years flashed past him like a video on fast forward.

Payton the beautiful young American intern. Payton dressed in a daring one sleeve silver gown at the Trussardis. Dancing with Payton and watching her eyes light as she laughed.

Leaning back against the window, he pushed open the shutter and stared at the garden bathed in moonlight.

The garden reminded him of Marilena and smacking the window shutter with his palm he realized he'd forgotten to call her, forgotten to stop by after dinner as he'd promised.

Dammit.

His hand fell from the shutter and turning, he leaned against the wall and looked at Payton. "Is there any pain yet, anything that hurts?"

"No."

"Good." He shoved his hands in his trouser pockets, the weight of the world pressing on him. *Payton. Marilena. The girls. Business.* There weren't any easy answers in life, were there? No clear cut direction. No obvious solution. It all came down to listening to one's conscience. To following one's heart.

"I know you had a plan," he said at length. "When you came here you had an idea of how you wanted this to go. What is it that you want? How can I help you?"

He listened to her, heard her out, and then when she was finally done talking he nodded. "Fine."

Marco had never appeared on Marilena's doorstep unannounced, and rarely before noon, but if the princess was surprised to see him at nine the next morning she gave no indication. "*Buongiorno,*" she said, when the maid showed Marco in.

"*Buongiorno, mia Amore,*" he answered, kissing each cheek. "How is your head today?"

"*Bene.*" She smiled. Fine.

His gaze traveled her pale face before resting on her bruised forehead. "Your black eye is getting worse."

"It gets uglier before it gets better," she answered,

making space for him on the small sofa in her private salon. "But I deserve a bump on my head if I'm going to run stoplights. It was stupid of me."

The maid soon returned with two small coffees on a gold tray. "How are things at home?" Marilena asked, cradling her cup.

"Fine." He looked up and discovered she'd been watching him, her smooth forehead slightly furrowed.

"Something's wrong," Marilena said softly.

There was no easy way to do this, no easy way to say this. Marilena was too intelligent, too perceptive to know that his news would change everything.

"Yes?" she prompted gently. And yet there was a new light in her eyes, wariness. Caution.

"Payton's sick." He didn't know how else to break the news. It was difficult to say without skirting the issue. "She has cancer."

Marilena's lips parted, eyes widening. "Cancer?"

"Yes."

"The poor thing."

And Marco felt like a heel all over again. He was doing the right thing, telling Marilena, letting Marilena know that he had to support Payton as much as possible, and yet he knew this was hard for her, just as this would be difficult for all of them.

"And the girls," Marilena added, correctly naming his chief worry. "Do they know? What will they do?"

He patted his coat, itching like mad for a cigarette. "They don't know yet, and—" He muttered an oath, hating all of this, hating the hard decisions that would soon have to be made. "Yet I know what Payton wants."

He glanced up, met Marilena's gaze. "She wants the girls to stay with me."

Marilena didn't move. Didn't blink. She just stared at him. "Stay with you? Payton, too?"

"No, not Payton. Just the girls. Payton wants us—you and me—to keep them while she goes through chemotherapy."

"Oh." Marilena stood, took a slow turn around the room, her long legs even more elegant in her slim slacks and high leather heels. "Good Heavens."

"Yes."

She turned a little, rubbed her temple and looked at him. "What do you think?"

"I think Payton's terrified. She loves the girls dearly. They're practically her whole world—"

"She does have a job, Marco. A very visible job as a designer for Calvanti."

"But she's taking a leave of absence. She's not going to try to work, at least not during the first part of her treatment, and she can't imagine lying around the house sick and having the girls be part of this."

"She's certainly been candid with you, hasn't she?"

"She's desperate."

Marilena blew a slow stream of air. "So, what are you proposing? What about the wedding? The honeymoon? Us?"

"We're still us. We'll still be us. We might need to make some changes." He saw her smooth brow knit and her teeth catch her lip. "But in the end everything will work out. We'll get married, have our trip. It just might be a few weeks—months—later than we planned.''

''But we'd have the twins.''

''Yes.''

''Before our honeymoon or after?''

He felt a surge of irritation. ''Does it matter?'' And then he saw from her expression that it did.

He straightened a little, a strange coldness forming in the middle of his chest. ''You don't want the girls?''

She held her breath a moment before answering. ''They're charming girls. Delightful children. But I've always hoped to be a bride before a mother.''

He didn't say anything and she calmly continued. ''I'm happy to help Payton however I can, but I think we have to be careful. I think we have to remember our goals. We've always talked about us starting a family together. Having babies of our own.''

But the twins *were* his own. They were a huge part of his heart. Of his life. They were *his* daughters.

Marilena turned on the sofa and placed a hand on his sleeve. ''I'm happy to be a stepmother. I have no problem watching them on holidays and weekends, but Marco, think about it. Becoming a full-time mother to children that are not my own, and *American!* It isn't practical. It doesn't make sense.''

Marco reached for his keys. ''I need to get back.''

''Marco.'' She pressed a swift kiss to his cheek. ''I want to get married. I want to be your wife. We have a plan, *si?*''

But the plan, he thought numbly heading for his car, might just be the wrong one.

Marco returned to the villa and headed into the house. He discovered Payton and the girls in the dining room still eating breakfast.

The heavy drapes had been drawn. The morning sun gleamed on the polished table. Cheery daisies spilled from a watering can. It was incongruous, the weedlike flowers in the watering can on his seventeenth-century dining table, and yet somehow it was right from the trio of heads sitting at the table, three heads of ringlets, Payton's dark auburn and the girls glossy black.

And Marilena's words came back to him as he stood in the doorway, *"They're not my own and they're American."*

Payton looked up, caught sight of him there and her mouth curved, blue eyes a little red from what he guessed had been a sleepless night, and yet there was more warmth in her expression than twenty average women put together.

He rather liked his Americans, he thought, as he entered the large formal room.

He was glad his daughters were half-American. Half-Payton. She might not be perfect but he liked her. Despite everything that had happened between them he still liked her very much.

Payton had never felt so insignificant sitting at the enormous table and yet Marco's sudden appearance energized the room. The large empty space no longer felt empty but full of life and vitality.

"Where did you find the flowers?" he asked, dropping his keys on a side console.

"The girls picked them on our walk this morning."

His eyebrows rose. "You've already been out on a walk?"

"To the soccer field at the park." Payton glanced at the girls who were suddenly very attentive. "We thought you'd left for the office already."

"I had an errand I needed to run, but I thought I'd have breakfast with you three first." He pulled out a chair near them and sat down. The maid instantly appeared with a glass of juice and a basket of warm rolls for Marco. *"Grazie,"* he said, thanking the young housemaid.

Payton watched him lightly butter the breakfast roll. "It's going to be warm today," she said, feeling a need to fill the silence. "I thought it'd be fun to take the girls out. We're planning an outing."

"We're going to a carnival," Gia added, rising on her knees.

"I didn't know a carnival was in town," Marco answered.

Payton nodded. "It's the annual festival held at the Navigli canals. You took me once some years ago and I thought the girls would enjoy the performers."

"It's June already?"

"Yes. It's summer," Liv chimed. "Can you come with us?"

He smiled at the girls, and with his sleeves rolled up on his tan forearms he looked remarkably relaxed for a man who'd slept little the night before. "I have another idea,'' he said. "What if we went to my favorite place in the whole world?''

"Where's that?'' Gia demanded.

"Capri.'' He glanced at Payton, and their gazes locked and held. "We'll all go,'' he said decisively as if he expected her to argue. "We'll spend a week relaxing together. I think we could use some sun, fresh air, and a change of pace.''

She was upstairs packing, trying to stay focused on the task at hand as Marco had said they'd be leaving later that afternoon, but it was hard to concentrate when her conscience pricked her.

Marco had said they'd fly to Naples, overnight in the city, and then either take a water taxi or helicopter to Capri the next day, but Payton couldn't ask him to do this. It wasn't right that he had to drop everything just for her.

As if able to read her thoughts, Marco stopped by the bedroom. "Nearly done?'' he asked.

"No, not by a long shot. I'm having trouble getting everything together.''

"Why? You're usually so organized.''

Payton turned from the dresser, her eyes wide with worry. "I can't help thinking that this isn't such a good idea.''

"What's not?''

Oh, did he have to play dense now? She suppressed a weary sigh. "The trip,'' she said. "The four of us going to Capri together. I know you have so much work. I know you're practically buried in it. Why don't you leave us in Naples. The girls and I can take a boat over to Capri together.''

"Leave you in Naples? Not a chance. This is a family trip. We'll all go.'' Marco's voice exuded authority, decisiveness. "Besides, you'll need me there. I should be there.'' He corrected himself. "I *want* to be there.''

This was the Marco who inspired such confidence. This was the man who knew what mattered and when.

Payton sagged with relief. She could literally feel the shift in energy. When she first arrived he'd been so hard with her, so distant, disinterested, but the cold wall was lifting, giving her a glimpse of light and warmth.

He'd come through for the girls. He'd do right by the girls. She didn't have to worry so much. Things were going to be fine. But still, there was his work and the looming fall show. "What about the collection?''

"It's not important.''

That wasn't true. The Spring collection was the heart of the business. "I'm not going to die tomorrow, Marco. You can't drop everything. Promise me you'll see the collection through.''

He stared at her hard. "Does it mean so much to you?''

"You have a gift. You're a visionary. I'd hate to come between you and your work.''

His brows pulled, lowering above his eyes as he considered her. The room felt charged. Payton found the tension almost unbearable.

"I don't understand you," he said at last. "But then, I never did."

He turned away, gazed out the window, but his face was blank, no hint of emotion in his hard yet sensual features. "If it'll give you peace of mind, I'll continue with the collection. I can handle most details via phone and modem, and if necessary, I'll fly back for last minute fittings."

"Thank you."

He turned to face her, his expression one of disbelief. "Why do you thank me?"

Her slim shoulders lifted. "You've been really good about all this. Very kind."

"Kind? *Santo Cielo!*" Marco swore softly. "I am not kind. I am far from kind. What I do is not kindness. It is necessity. It is the only thing I can do."

Still. She was gratified and comforted more than he'd ever know. It was a relief to know that Marco understood and accepted the challenge. The girls would need so much in the coming months, they'd need strength and courage as well as endless love.

"This—" she picked the words delicately "—will change many things."

"I'm aware of that."

"And Marilena—"

"She knows."

"She's okay with you taking us?"

"She's fine, Payton."

Her heart squeezed tight with a bittersweet pain that was more bitter than anything. "I'm sorry, Marco—"

"Do not apologize for this. You did not want this,

you haven't asked for this, I do not want you to ever apologize for something beyond your control.''

''But it impacts *you*.''

''*Bene.* So be it. I'm a man, Payton, not a child. I expect life to be difficult. I accept that there will be challenges. Disappointments.'' His dark eyes met hers and they glowed with hot emotion. ''But I do not accept defeats. You will beat this, Payton, and life will go on.''

CHAPTER SEVEN

NAPLES was beautiful any time of day and Payton was lucky to see the city in the afternoon sun and then witness it come alive late at night, too.

Arriving in Naples, they checked into a lavish suite in the luxury hotel, Excelsior, which overlooked the sparkling bay and boasted views of Mount Vesuvius beyond.

After changing into comfortable shoes and clothes they set off to explore the city, the streets of old Naples like all the other tourists.

Marco was passionate about Naples and he loved showing the city off. His late mother was a true Neapolitan and he'd spent many of his early years visiting his grandparents and aunts and uncles in and around Naples, including the Amalfi Coast.

With the girls comfortably seated in strollers, Marco and Payton toured some of the famous cathedrals and churches before exploring Castel Nuovo, a massive thirteenth century fortress which became the royal palace of the powerful fifteenth century Aragons.

No wonder Naples had been called Italy's 'most beautiful crown', Payton thought, as they left the cool, dark chambers of the Palazzo Reale and stepped into glorious sunshine. There was so much cultural history here beginning with the ancient Greek and

Roman civilizations, so many architectural master-pieces, and an abundance of natural beauty as well.

But the afternoon of walking and sightseeing had worn the little ones out and even Payton craved a nap before they headed to dinner.

Marco had booked a two-bedroom suite and back at the hotel Payton put the girls down for a nap in one room before returning to the living room. "I know you'd like a rest, too," Marco said. "Take the bedroom. I'll sleep in here tonight."

"I'm not going to have you sleeping on a couch when you're paying for the rooms."

"I could care less about the money," he answered impatiently. "Why do you do that? Why do you even bring up money?"

He muttered something, clearly irritated and opened his address book as if to make a phone call but he didn't reach for the phone. "Money can buy a lot of things but it can't buy happiness or peace of mind. And that's what we need most right now. Calm and quiet. A restful week with our children."

When focused, no one rivaled Marco's determination or drive. This was the Marco she believed in, and trusted. "I agree."

Slightly mollified, he sat back in his chair at the desk. "Have you thought about when you'll tell the girls what is happening?"

"No."

"You can't leave them in the dark. It's not right. Wouldn't be fair."

"Well, I'm certainly not going to tell them that I'm sick, that I have the same sickness my mother did, and my aunt. They know what happened to them. I won't have the girls worrying.''

"But they'll worry regardless.''

"Which is why I need you to make them feel extra loved, extra wanted. I know that you have a lot going on right now, and I know I'm adding another burden—''

"Jesus, Payton!'' he interrupted, swearing violently. "Do I have to ring your neck? What kind of unfeeling monster do you think I am? The girls are *not* a burden. They've never been a burden, and for that matter,'' he shot her a savage glance, "neither have you.''

This statement was met by profound silence. Payton's head felt a bit fuzzy, as is she couldn't see her way clear through the stream of words to the meaning.

"The whole marriage thing—our *marriage*,'' Marco clarified grimly, "was not the great tragedy you seem to think it was. I never saw marrying you as a negative thing. It became difficult later, but not initially. I wouldn't have married you if I'd found the idea abhorrent.''

"But—''

"But nothing. I would not have married you if I hadn't had feelings for you. I would not have married you just to be correct.''

Feelings. Payton blinked, not certain if she should laugh or cry. He'd had feelings when he married her. Was that good, or was that bad? And if the feelings had been good, why hadn't their marriage lasted?

"You've done a good job with the girls,'' he added

more quietly. "They'll miss you if you leave them in Milan."

Her eyes felt gritty. "I'll miss them, too. But I think it's better if they don't see me when I'm not at my best. I think it's better if they don't have to see me go through the side effects."

He didn't say anything for a long moment. He rubbed his jaw and then shook his head before abruptly rising. "I'm going to postpone the wedding."

"No!"

He shrugged off her protest. "There's no way I could get married and go on a long honeymoon now. My daughters will need me near and Marilena is a woman, an adult. She understands complications. The children don't. It's the children I'm worried about. In the light of your illness, all other problems become insignificant."

"You should at least talk to Marilena before you make this decision."

"Whether I do or don't, I've made the decision. The girls are my priority. The girls, Payton, must come first."

She smiled faintly. "You would have been a wonderful emperor in ancient Rome."

"I know." Then he smiled, too, and grooves formed next to his mouth. He was mocking himself and when Marco laughed at himself like this he was at his most charming. "Now get some sleep. You should rest while the girls are quiet. And don't worry about me in here. I'm fine. I have plenty of work to do anyway."

Shutting the bedroom door behind her, Payton stretched out on the queen-size bed. Her head ached, her heart ached, she felt as though she were on fire. It was getting harder and harder to be around Marco and keep things light, casual. It was harder to keep perspective. Harder to keep her heart in check.

As difficult as it would be to leave the girls behind, it'd be so much easier once she'd put distance between her and Marco.

Marco still had that crazy effect on her where she felt so much, wanted so much, craved so much.

It was awful playing this game, awful hiding all her feelings, squashing them down until her heart ached endlessly.

It'd been less than a week since she arrived in Milan and already she felt wrung out. It was getting harder to act nonchalant around him, harder to deny the intensity of her feelings. She hated having to pretend she didn't love him, or that she felt nothing everytime she heard his voice, or his name.

How to ignore the leap of her heart? How to numb hope? How to behave as though she didn't mind that Marco belonged to another woman? Because she did mind. Very much. She loved Marco, but she hadn't forgotten the excruciating failed marriage, either.

In the end Payton couldn't sleep and she finally left the bedroom to join Marco on the balcony. The sun was rapidly disappearing in a gorgeous red and purple sunset.

Marco ordered a bottle of wine and something to eat from room service, and an exquisite tray of meats, marinated vegetables, and selection of cheeses was promptly delivered to their suite.

"What's this?" Payton asked as Marco opened the bottle of red wine.

If she didn't know him better, she'd say Marco was being romantic, setting the scene for seduction. But she did know him and she knew he didn't have romantic or sexual feelings for her.

They stood on their hotel balcony and watched the sun sink into the ocean. It was a rare moment of tranquillity, she thought. It'd been ages since she felt any peace. She'd had so much worry on her mind for so long. "This is nice," she said, standing beside Marco, leaning on the railing.

"It is," he agreed.

Yet as the sun's red glow faded, Payton couldn't help the twinge of regret. She didn't have much time left with the girls. She'd be leaving Italy in a week's time. The girls would adjust to life without her—but would she?

How would she handle an empty house day after day after day? There'd be no one to come home to. No one to get up for. No one to kiss good-night.

"That's a heavy sigh," Marco said, looking at her, the evening breeze ruffling his dark hair.

"I've been thinking about my life lately, about all the mistakes I've made." She turned her head, looked at him. "I've made a lot of mistakes."

"Who hasn't?"

"I'm not talking business."

A muscle pulled at his jaw. "Neither am I." He reached behind her, lifted the bottle of wine from the table and topped off their glasses. "Want to talk mistakes? I shouldn't have let you return to California with the girls. It was the worst thing I could have done.

"I missed them so much it hurt," he continued. "Visiting you made it worse. Every time I got on the plane to come home I couldn't breathe. I felt like—" he looked away, features tightening "—like I was being buried alive."

"So you stopped coming."

"It was better staying away than saying goodbye over and over again." He took a quick drink from his glass. "But it wasn't the right thing to do. I failed them. And I failed you. I'm sorry."

His apology lingered in his mind long after they headed inside to dress for dinner before waking the girls. Payton slipped into white silk trousers and a turquoise silk peasant blouse with full sleeves and a drawstring neck. Once dressed, they took the elevator to the restaurant on the top of the hotel for dinner.

Although it was last minute and they had no reservation, the maître d' recognized Marco and seated them right away in a prime seat by the window. Situated on the top floor, La Terrazza had amazing views of the city, port, and mountain and the girls were entertained during the meal watching the large cruise ships arrive and depart from the harbor.

Marco suddenly reached out and covered her hand with his. "This is right, what we're doing. Going to Capri together. Putting aside our differences. If you have any doubts at all, just look at our daughters."

She'd been thinking the same thing and she shivered, moved not just by his touch, but his words. He understood, she thought, more than she'd given him credit for.

But when he lifted her hand to his mouth and kissed the back of her fingers, she felt a thrill that had nothing to do with maternal devotion or protective instinct. The warmth of his mouth against her skin made her hot and made her want.

Despite everything she was still a woman, and in the past two years there had been no one. No one to touch her. No one to love her. She hadn't wanted anyone but Marco and yet he wasn't hers to have.

His eyes met hers. "Capri is just what you need." He turned her hand over, kissed the inside of her wrist. His lips felt like fire on the wild beating of her pulse. "It might just be what I need, too."

She'd spent so much time boxing up her feelings, shutting down her emotions, and yet it only took a moment for Marco to undo all her carefully constructed control.

Pull away, she told herself, as heat rushed through her, heat and desire which threatened to crumble the last of her resistance. And somehow she did.

In the morning as they were checking out of the hotel, Marco's cell phone rang. "Marilena," he said, answering the call. He moved away a little bit and Payton stood with the girls and their suitcases near the lobby door waiting for the taxi that would carry them to the port.

Payton didn't hear much of the conversation. She didn't want to hear much of the conversation and she intentionally busied herself playing a game counting red cars with the girls to keep her focus out on the street instead of on Marco.

Marco glanced at Payton from beneath his lashes as he listened to Marilena describe a party he'd missed the night before. "Everyone asked about you," the princess said. "You were definitely missed."

"I'll be back in a week," he answered, wondering why he felt so irritated. He and Marilena had always been so social together; they were quite a power couple in their strata-sphere.

"How is it going? How was your night in Naples?"

"The girls enjoyed Naples," he answered, watching Payton crouch beside the girls at the glass window. It looked almost as if they were playing a game and Payton was laughing as Gia and Livia argued over who'd gotten the last point. "We had dinner at La Terazza."

"You took the children to La Terazza? But darling, it's not a restaurant for children."

"They behaved beautifully." He saw the taxi pull up and the hotel doorman gestured to Payton. "I need to go," he said. "Our taxi is here. I don't want to miss our shuttle to Capri."

"All right, darling, call me soon. Bye bye."

The taxi whisked them from the hotel to the bay and they arrived at the port just in time to board one of the high-speed hydrofoils that would carry them to Capri. It was only a forty-minute ride, Marco explained. Hundreds of tourists made the round trip every day in summer.

The hydrofoil picked up speed and Payton watched the steep hillsides with the cascade of pastel houses recede. Naples from the water was even more spectacular. Indeed the whole coastline—all green and blue and jewel tone colors—sparkled in the sun.

As Naples dwindled from the view, Payton thought back to the dream she'd had in high school. The dream had been to come to Italy, to see the great art and cathedrals of ancient Rome. She'd wanted to take an apartment in Milan and study fashion with the top designers. She'd longed to drink coffee and watch the sun rise over the land where great art and great minds had given the world culture.

An hour later, the hydrofoil pulled alongside the harbor and the crew turned to the task of docking. The sun felt warmer already.

Marco suddenly leaned forward and kissed Payton's forehead, his hand tangling in her long loose curls. ''You look happy,'' he said. ''It's good to see you smile.''

She blushed, heat blooming through her middle at his touch.

He dipped his head again and this time kissed her cheek, near her mouth. She smelled the spice of his cologne—his own signature fragrance, *Marco,* which sold like mad in the States, felt the rough edge of his beard despite the fact that he'd shaved earlier that morning, felt his warmth from the dazzling Italian sun.

She could feel him, smell him, and it all seemed

surreal. Funny how everything could change but nothing changed. But everything had changed. Marco was not hers. Even if the wedding had been postponed, he was still promised to another woman. He still belonged to another woman.

Marco's hand slid from her hair and she ducked beneath his arm, took a quick step away. It'd been two years since their divorce. She'd had two years to accept reality.

So why couldn't she? Why couldn't she accept that she no longer had a future with Marco? And why on earth didn't the pain—and longing—go away?

"What's wrong?" he demanded.

"Nothing." Dammit. She couldn't do this, couldn't start feeling all these old feelings again. She'd worked so hard to shut down her emotions, to bottle up the want and need. Yet being around him was making her feel so much and what she felt terrified her.

There was only one man for her. Only Marco, and yet Marco wasn't an option.

His house wasn't actually in Capri, but Anacapri, on the other side of the massive mountain. It was built on a slope above the ocean and it sprawled in elegant terraces. Flowers cascaded over the balconies and more flowers surrounded the pool on the lower terrace.

With Liv in one arm and Gia in the other, Marco gave her the grand tour. The house had been his mother's, and his grandparents before. His mother's family had come to Anacapri for generations and although they were less than a mile from downtown

Capri, Marco's neighborhood felt peaceful, almost rural.

In Payton's bedroom he opened the door to the balcony and walked outside into the sunshine. Marco drew a deep breath and exhaled. The girls giggled.

"Smell the air here," he said. "Feel the sun. Isn't this wonderful?"

Payton couldn't tear her gaze away from him. It was wonderful. It was wonderful and awful and she didn't know how she'd survive the next seven days alone with him.

The girls were here but in some ways the girls made it harder. The girls were a constant reminder that she and Marco had been close once. Intimate. They'd made love.

Payton closed her eyes, took a steadying breath. She couldn't let herself think about making love, couldn't let herself remember how amazing it had been with Marco.

His touch had been perfect. His hands knew how to touch her. His body felt like heaven against hers.

She'd heard from friends that sex the first time wasn't always pleasurable. She'd heard that it sometimes took practice—experience—for the physical act to make physical and emotional sense.

It hadn't been like that with Marco. The first time had been incredible. She'd cried when he'd moved inside her, cried at the intense pleasure, the unbelievable sensation of him in her, of him with her.

When he brought her to an orgasm she cried yet again and Payton knew, despite her limited experience, that she'd never be with anyone else who made her feel this way, and decided then that if she couldn't be with Marco, she'd rather be with no one.

"It is wonderful," she said after a moment, turning to smile at the girls and Marco, doing her best to hide the heartache.

Marco set the girls on their feet. "This island is magical. It has the power to heal, the power to make whole."

Payton's heart turned inside out. "Enough for a miracle?"

His intense gaze met hers and held. "Without a doubt."

CHAPTER EIGHT

THEY spent the first couple of days acting like tourists, visiting the popular spots with the throng of Americans and Europeans visitors who'd taken the boat over from the mainland for the day.

Finally, though, Marco had enough of the tourist crush and suggested a picnic away from the crowds and frenzied shoppers in town.

To the girls' delight, they took one of Capri's rambling buses and bumped along the road until Marco signaled to the driver that they wanted off.

The driver dropped them just above the Villa Damecuta. The villa had once been one of Tiberius' twelve imperial villas on Capri but was nothing more than ruins now. Yet the ruins had a spectacular view of the water and offered a perfect spot for picnics.

Payton spread the blanket out on a grassy knoll and they munched on sandwiches and drank lemonade before the girls set out to explore.

Payton followed the girls and then sat down on what was left of an old stone wall. Marco took a seat next to her. The sunshine was glorious. The day was glorious.

''You couldn't ask for more perfect weather,'' he said, leaning back a little, arms braced behind him.

She turned her head and smiled. He was wearing a navy knit shirt, sleeves pushed up to his elbows and it was a very casual look but very sexy. "I think heaven must be like this." Her smile faltered a fraction, suddenly self-conscious.

She looked back at the twins who were oblivious to all, intent on their game of hopscotch among the ruins. "The girls are so happy here. You must bring them here again. Promise me."

"Of course. Capri is my second home. The house here has been in my mother's family for generations." He leaned forward, adjusted her hat to better shield her face. "You don't talk about your mother much. Why?"

"It's difficult." Payton was grateful for the straw hat's brim. His gentleness, his protectiveness, was still so new. She wasn't accustomed to a tender Marco.

"She had cancer, too, didn't she?" Marco persisted.

Talking about her mother wasn't much easier than contemplating her own future but Marco would need to know these things. Someone should tell the girls about their mother's family. "I loved my mom," she said simply. "We were very close. It was just the two of us growing up. Dad left years ago—he remarried and has another family somewhere—so it's been Mom and me for almost as long as I can remember."

"You never heard from your dad after he left?"

She shrugged. "He sent a Christmas card announcing he was getting married and then that was the end of that."

He reached over and plucked a loose curl from the edge of her hat and tucked it beneath the brim, behind her ear. "I have a feeling your mom would be proud of you. I imagine you're a lot like her."

Payton loved the feel of his hand against her ear and cheek. She loved it when he touched her but he didn't touch her often. It wasn't just a skin thing; it was a heart thing.

Marco stood and reaching for her hand, pulled Payton to her feet. "I'm sorry now I never had the chance to meet your mother. I think I would have liked her."

"You would have driven each other crazy."

"Just like you've driven me crazy." Marco's eyes glowed as he gazed down at her. He still held her hand in his, fingers loosely linked.

"I never drove you crazy! You hardly knew I existed."

But the moment the words were out of her mouth, Payton felt a tingle race down her spine. His gaze was intense and she felt a rise of energy, the tension back between them.

"I'm glad you and the girls are back," he said, voice husky as his head dipped and he kissed her gently, on her cheek near her mouth.

Her heart began to thud and blood raced through her. She felt a wash of hot desire. The awareness of him, of her, of the energy of them together, was almost too much for her to bear.

"We can't do this." She placed her against his chest to push him away but once her hand made contact with his chest she couldn't move, couldn't escape. He felt big, strong, hard. He felt like the Marco she loved, the Marco she'd missed.

"Marilena," Payton whispered, her throat growing parched. "There's Marilena."

He lifted her chin, stared down into her eyes. "Fine. I'll end it with her then."

Payton's heart jumped to her throat. The adrenaline was making her tremble, her legs so weak they felt disconnected from the rest of her. "You can't do that. You can't do that to her. Not again, not—"

He lowered his head and covered her mouth with his, silencing her protest with a real kiss.

She'd stiffened, instinctively resisting, but his lips were warm, persuasive and the firm pressure of his mouth sent sparks of feeling throughout her body. It was hard to deny her hunger, much less her attraction. His breath, his touch, his skin—it was all so familiar and yet strange, wonderful and yet heartbreaking.

No one had ever made her feel as much as Marco, and yet Marco didn't belong to her. This kiss, like everything else between them, was stolen. Fleeting. He'd be gone, back to Milan in no time and she'd be on her own again. Struggling to put together the pieces of her life.

She tried to shut down her emotions, limit her response, but it was as if he knew her struggle and was determined to prove her desire was stronger than her common sense.

He deepened the kiss, his lips parting hers and even as she shuddered at the flick of his tongue, Marco reached up to cup her breast through her thin knit summer top.

Payton inhaled sharply as fingers closed around one taut nipple and rubbed the sensitive flesh. He was making her want things, want him, and it was impossible. It couldn't happen. They both had to have more control.

"Stop," she breathed against his mouth. "Stop, stop, Marco, this is wrong. You know it. I know it. We can't do this."

He lifted his head, stared down at her. He was breathing just as hard as she. "Then maybe it's time we made some changes."

She clenched her hands, pushed against his chest. "Don't. I didn't come to interfere. I don't want to interfere. We've done this before. Tried this before. It didn't work, remember? You divorced me, Marco—"

"Only because you asked me to."

Payton couldn't do this. She didn't want to do this. "I asked you to divorce me if you weren't ever going to love me, and you said—" she swallowed, fighting to hang on to her composure, as well as her pride, "I was a mistake," she persisted, her voice breaking. "A...one-night stand. Or don't you remember that, too?"

Of course he remembered the words. They'd been cruel. "I lied." The words had been deliberately cruel. He'd lashed out at her, trying to get back at her. Her unhappiness made him crazy. Nothing he did was right. Nothing was good enough.

"I lied," he repeated, just as he realized he'd been lying to himself ever since. "You were never a one-night stand. You—*we*—weren't a mistake, either."

"No."

"Yes. We were inevitable. We were meant to happen."

*   *   *

Marco had hoped he could manage business from Capri but there were too many issues requiring his input. He might be able to have fabric samples sent to him, but they couldn't do proper fittings or final model interviews without his approval.

"I'm going to Milan," he announced the next morning. "I'll catch a flight from Naples and probably won't be able to make it back until tomorrow late afternoon."

It was nearly noon when he reached Milan but instead of heading straight to his showroom in the fashion district, he had his driver take him by Marilena's house.

"It's good to see you," Marilena said, warmly welcoming him. "I've missed you."

But he hadn't missed her. In fact, he hadn't even thought of her unless Payton brought her up.

He was doing the right thing, breaking off the engagement. His heart had only ever loved one woman and that was the redhead in Capri.

Marco waited for Marilena to take a seat. Marilena sat down gracefully. She was remarkably elegant, even in times of duress, but her leisurely movements grated on him today for the first time. He knew without a doubt he and Marilena were over. Their relationship had run its course. Marilena was a beautiful woman but she wasn't the right woman for him. The past two years he'd felt like a man sleepwalking through life and suddenly he was awake at last.

Thank God Payton had arrived when she had.
Thank God he hadn't made Marilena his wife.

"We need to talk," he said. He'd never loved
Marilena. He'd loved the idea that a beautiful, desir-
able woman like the princess would want him. But
he'd never loved Marilena, at least, not the way he
loved Payton.

He told her as much, too, and Marilena's composure began to crack. "You said she wouldn't come
between us. You insisted she wouldn't ruin the wedding." She never raised her voice, never lost control
but she sounded close to breaking down now.
"Marco, don't let her do this."

"She's not the one—"

"How can you say that? Things were fine, things
were perfect, before she came."

He sighed, closed his eyes. "Things weren't fine.
We were pretending."

"I wasn't," she retorted fiercely. "I do love you.
I know we could have a great life together. We are
so similar, you and me, we understand each other.
Suit each other. How can you forget everything we've
shared these past two years?"

"We've had fun," he agreed, knowing that they
both had loved the opera, the shopping trips to Paris,
the escapes to Rome for dinner with mutual friends.
"But it's not enough."

"How can you say that?"

"Because it's true. There are the children to think
of," he said. "You've already it would be too much
to take responsibility for them while Payton starts her
treatment."

Marilena stood, walked to the end of the salon and averting her face wiped the traces of tears. "You will be sorry. You'll regret this decision especially when you realize she's tricked you again."

"Payton's not like that—"

"You're such a fool!" Marilena turned to face him, her lovely face twisted in pain. "She *is* like that. She *is* manipulative. Destructive. She's only here because you're getting married again. She's here to break us up and I have to hand it to her. She's succeeded. She's got you right back in the palm of her hand."

The princess' expression suddenly darkened. "You haven't—" she broke off, swallowed, her pale complexion going even whiter. "You haven't…been intimate have you?"

"No."

Her features crumpled yet again. "And I'm supposed to believe you?"

Her question offended him. He'd never seen her like this, never seen her so upset by anything. *"Yes,"* he answered quietly. "Take care of yourself, Marilena. I hope we can always be friends."

After Marco left Capri for Milan that morning, Payton and the girls spent the day at the villa's elegant pool surrounded by pots of cascading purple bougainvillea. They swam, had lunch on the terrace, then played again in the shady end of the pool before taking a long lazy afternoon nap.

The day had been delightfully relaxed, but the next morning Payton felt restless. When she was with

Marco she didn't think so much, or worry so much, but with him gone all her fears came rushing back.

Hard to believe she had it. The *C* word. Cancer.

She knew the steps that would come, knew how the treatment would go, she'd been through his before, not just once, but twice. Her mother. Her mother's sister.

Payton drew a breath, pictured only positive outcomes, unlike her mother and Aunt Susie's outcome. She'd beat it.

She'd come through it okay. And if she didn't, well, the girls would be with their father.

That was positive, right?

But thinking positive didn't ease all her fears, nor did it dull the ache inside her. She missed Marco. A lot. She missed his face, his smile, his voice, his touch. She missed the way he walked into a room, the way he swung the girls into his arms, the way he looked at her over the top of the twins' heads.

But the very fact that she felt so much, craved his company this much, sounded a warning inside her.

She was getting far too attached. She was seriously falling for him all over again.

Nothing good would come of this, she reminded herself, vigorously brushing her hair. He wasn't hers. She wasn't his type. Hadn't she learned anything from last time?

Eyes stinging, Payton forced herself to action, twisting her dark red curls into a knot on top of her head before gathering keys, wallet, and loose change, depositing all in her bright orange and red striped leather bag.

She collected the girls from the nursery. Thank God for the twins. She adored their chatter, their high spirits, their sense of fun. Like her, they loved adventurers.

Outside, Gia's hand in her left and Liv's in her right, they strolled down the street hop-hopping every third step at Gia's insistence.

"Mommy," Liv's small voice trilled in the golden sunshine.

"Yes, sweetheart?"

"Where are we going?"

"Shopping. Playing," Payton answered thinking that the sun was gorgeous, glorious yellow light, and the leaves on the trees shone vibrant green.

She drew a breath, reveling in the fullness of the afternoon, telling herself that this—it—was all…the highest, the best, the girls the three of them together in beautiful Capri. What more could one ask for?

Life.

"That's it?" Livia persisted.

"Maybe the hair salon." Payton hated the sudden squeeze of her chest, the air pinched as if caught in a fist. "And then we'll get some ice cream."

Gia stopped hop-hopping, and pulled the others to a stop, too. "Are we getting our hair cut?"

It's not a big deal, Payton reminded herself. This is minor. In the big picture hair means nothing. "No, sweet pea. Just Mommy is getting her hair cut."

"Cut?" Liv chimed.

"Yes, shortened for the winter, I think."

Gia's forehead wrinkled and she gazed up and

about at the cloudless blue sky with the endless sunshine. "But it's not winter, Mommy."

"No, but it will be and I thought I'd simplify things. Besides, change is good."

Despite Payton's cheerful tone, the girls gazed at her wide-eyed, pensive, their easiness gone.

"Short like Gramma's?" Gia challenged.

Payton held her smile although her jaw had begun to ache. "I'm sure there are other short styles that aren't quite so severe, don't you think?"

Liv's dark blue eyes watered. "But Mommy I love your hair. You have bea-u-tiful hair."

"Thank you, baby. You have beautiful hair, too." And Payton hugged the girls, touched, pained.

She didn't want this, either, but far better she do the big chop at once then watch her hair fall out in clumps, and far better the girls know about it in advance then it be some secret shock later. "Well, you two come with me and help me pick out a new style. It'll be fun. You'll be my advisors, right?"

They were walking again and the sunlight dappled the pavement but the girls had lost some of their exuberance. Livia clung tightly to Payton's hand and Gia shot her mother curious side glances.

"Mommy," Gia said after a moment. "Will your hair grow back?"

Payton squeezed Gia's hand. "Of course."

The girls reluctantly let the subject go and they walked the rest of the way talking about more cheerful subjects.

Entering town, they crossed the wide square with the beautiful stone plaza. Flowers bloomed everywhere, riots of color in huge glazed planters and friendly wrought iron window baskets.

They were just a block from the stylish hair salon when Livia stretched out an arm and cried, "Look! Daddy! He's back!"

Payton felt a thrill as Marco headed their way. "You're back early. We didn't expect you until later tonight."

"Wrapped up things sooner than I expected," he answered, swinging the twins up into his arms. He leaned over to kiss Payton but she nervously turned her head, giving him her cheek instead of her mouth.

She saw the flicker in his eyes, her cheek wasn't what he'd wanted. From his expression she didn't know whether he was angry or amused, but he dutifully kissed her cheek and let it slide. "Where are you three heading?"

Payton adjusted the straps of her oversized bag. "We're just running errands." She prayed the girls wouldn't say a word about the hair appointment. She knew Marco loved her hair long, but he wasn't the one who'd have to watch it fall out in clumps. "And then we're going to get an ice cream."

"Ice cream? You girls like ice cream?" Marco teased, grooves forming on either side of his mouth as he smiled at Gia and Liv.

"Yes!" the girls squealed in unison, delighted by the attention. They'd enjoyed getting to know Marco better. The starchy uneasiness had finally begun to disappear.

"Mommy's getting her hair cut," Liv announced solemnly.

Oh, damn. Payton hid her frustration with a bright smile but Marco wasn't buying it.

He looked at her through narrowed eyes. "She is?"

"Mmm, all off," Gia added sharply. *"Short."*

"I don't like short," Liv cried. "I like Mommy's hair long."

Marco set the girls down. "Well, then maybe Mommy doesn't have to cut her hair today."

Payton could feel his displeasure and instead of ducking his gaze, she lifted her chin and met it head on. This was her business, not his. The cancer was her cancer, not his. The treatment was hers as well. In the end she was the one sick. In the end it was her body under siege. "I have an appointment. I can't cancel at this late notice."

"Sure you can," Marco returned. "I'll cancel it for you and leave a generous tip. They won't complain. They understand things come up."

"Marco."

"No. This is the girls' vacation. *Our* vacation. You can do this later. In fact, it'd probably be easier later. For everyone involved."

She wanted to be angry with him. She wanted to show him—remind him—that she was independent and capable of making decisions on her own, but truthfully, she didn't want to upset the girls. Not this week. Not when she wanted to create lasting, happy memories.

So Marco canceled the appointment and then joined them on their errands around town. And Marco took their errands very seriously indeed. He read all the labels on the different sunblocks. He directed the shoe salesman toward the sandals he preferred, although in the end the twins got the pair they liked best. He tried hat after hat on Payton's head until he found the perfect one, with the brim not too small, not too floppy, and without any ridiculous flowers or ribbons.

Payton fought the urge to hurry him. Three simple errands had never taken so long and yet he obviously enjoyed being part of the shopping and selection process.

"Done?" she asked, after popping into a corner convenience store to pick up some sweets and fun magazines for Pietra, the young woman Marco had hired to help look after the girls.

"If you are," he answered.

"Yes."

"Then let's get ice cream!" the girls begged, drooping in the afternoon heat. "Now? Please?"

Marco agreed and they ducked into a semidark store where an old ceiling fan gently whirred and the air felt deliciously cool.

"Ah," Payton sighed, sinking into a delicate wrought iron chair. "It feels great in here."

"It's not that hot outside." Marco withdrew his wallet and paid for the girls' ice cream.

"I'm from San Francisco," she answered, pulling out a seat for Livia to sit down and then a chair for Gia. "When I'm not at work I live in sweatshirts."

"You glamour-puss."

Payton laughed. She liked it when Marco teased her. She liked it when things were easy between them…friendly. "I can't help that my ancestors were from the Nordic countries where everything was ice and snow.''

He returned to the table with a small cup of gelato for her. ''Thankfully there's no ice in your veins. You run about as hot as they come.''

Payton's head jerked up, heat suffusing her face. The caressing note in his voice knocked her off balance nearly as much as what he'd said.

''*Shh,*'' she hushed him, indicating the girls sitting at the table eating scoops of chocolate and vanilla ice cream.

He shrugged. ''They're focused on other things.''

''Still.''

''Still what?''

He'd leaned forward and his voice had dropped an octave. He was doing something to her, stirring her senses, not to mention her imagination. ''You shouldn't say such things.''

Marco reached over, borrowed her spoon for a taste of her coffee flavored ice cream. ''Why not?''

He looked up at her, dark eyes hot, interest shimmering. ''It's true.''

CHAPTER NINE

RETURNING from town, they all cooled off with a swim. Then Pietra put the girls down for a nap and Marco and Payton lingered at the pool.

As Marco stretched out on a towel in the sun, Payton settled in a chaise with a book. Yet as she stared at the page, the words didn't penetrate her brain. She sat rereading the same paragraph for the third time, thinking about everything but the novel.

It struck her that she'd been so focused on doing the right thing for the girls, keeping it all together for the family, she'd forgotten some of her needs had nothing to do with the world at large.

Some of her needs had absolutely nothing to do with duty, responsibility, or maturity.

Being around Marco was making her feel—even if she didn't want to feel. For the first time in ages she was aware of the old heat and fire, the whisper of want that Marco stirred inside of her.

She had expected the trip to Italy would drain her, deplete her. She'd expected anger and pain, frustration and regret, and while she'd felt some of that, she also felt more. She felt warmth. Fullness. Security. Perhaps the fullness and warmth wouldn't last forever, but it was reassuring to find it again.

It was rather wonderful to feel something intense and tangible again.

"It's getting hot," Marco said, rising. His body gleamed with perspiration, each hard muscle in his flat abdomen distinct.

She felt a ripple of desire in her middle, an attraction that wasn't just physical but emotional. Even if she wanted to ignore him, she couldn't. She felt him always, was aware of him always. It was almost as if she'd been wired from birth to know him.

To feel him.

To want him.

And she did want him, very much so. The intensity of her feelings scared her.

He dived back into the pool and she watched him swim laps. He was a good swimmer with a strong effective stroke and he covered the pool quickly, doing a dozen laps freestyle before flipping over and swimming another dozen on his back.

He pulled up at the end of the pool, not far from her chair and gave his head a toss, shaking the water from his hair. "Why would you take the girls for your haircut?" he asked, leaning on the pool's edge.

"Why wouldn't I? They've always gone with me to my hair appointments."

"Yes, but to cut your hair all the way off? It's pretty drastic."

"Chemo is pretty drastic."

"I've never known anyone who has gone through chemo."

Payton gave up all pretense of reading and tossed her book aside. "I've seen more of it than I ever wanted to see. It can save a life, but it's hard on the body. My mom's hair fell out in huge clumps. One day she had a head of hair. The next strands began to fall out. By the end of the week she'd had to shave her head.''

''So you thought if you cut your hair short now, it wouldn't be such a overwhelming change later.''

''Yes.''

He nodded slowly. ''These next six months will be very difficult on you, won't they?''

''Very,'' she agreed softly.

He looked up, smiled at her and yet his expression in his eyes was somber. ''Then I say we enjoy every minute of our time here so we both go home with unforgettable memories.''

Her heart lurched a bit. Time seemed so short. She'd never felt so mortal. ''That sounds great.''

''Let's start with dinner in Capri tonight,'' he said, toweling off. ''I'll make some reservations at a little place I like and this evening will be for just you and me.''

Marco waited outside by the taxi as Payton kissed the girls good night. He could see the twins hugging Payton, their arms wrapped tight around her waist. They absolutely adored her. And Payton was so good with them. She was firm and yet fun at the same time. She knew how to handle Gia's high spirits and Liv's sensitive nature.

Please, God, don't let anything happen to Payton.

She was heading his way now and he admired her casual yet chic elegance. She was wearing a beaded camisole—tiny black beaded flowers over delicate white silk—and black velvet slacks that sat low on her hips, the pant legs slightly flared. Her pale shoulders were bare and she wore high strappy sandals. It was a great look for her.

She had incredible style. Marilena knew how to dress, he thought, but Payton had fire.

Yet as Payton reached the taxi he saw her blue eyes were wet and her black lashes stuck together black and spikey.

He put his hand on her back. "What's wrong? What's happened?"

Payton looked at him, and tried to smile yet her full lips quivered and she couldn't mask her emotion. "It's nothing. I'm just thinking too much."

She caught a glimpse of the girls still standing Pietra on the villa's front steps with Pietra and she lifted her hand in a final wave. "I want to have forever with them," she said, struggling to hold back fresh tears. "I want to be well and strong and a good mother always."

He drew her against him, held her in his arms. "We'll get you well, I promise."

"But what if chemo doesn't work?" Her voice came out muffled. "What if I'm not there for them as they grow up? I can't bear it, Marco, I can't."

She shuddered and then drew a deep breath. "I'm sorry." Lifting her head she forced a watery smile. "We better go before I really scare the girls."

Marco was silent in the car and Payton felt worn out before the night had even begun. She glanced at him from the corner of her eye and he looked very grave and preoccupied.

"I don't know why I fell apart," she said, her voice

still husky. "Everything was fine. I was actually feeling very happy."

"You're going to beat this, Payton," he said,
reaching over and taking her hand. "You're strong.
Much stronger than you think."

"But if I don't, I know the girls will be fine with
you."

His hand squeezed hers. "No. They need you.
They'll always need you. So dammit, fight, Payton.
Beat this. You have to."

"I intend to."

The restaurant was in the middle of town, flanking
the charming Piazzetta. They were seated at an outside table in the colonnaded courtyard and strands of
white lights were strung above the courtyard and can-
dles glowed on each table.

The menu made Payton's mouth water. Ravioloi
all'Annibale—ricotta and herb stuffed ravilois served
with butter, sage and parmesan cheese. Penne alla
Cantinella—pasta with aubergines, tomato and moz-
zarella.

"I'm really hungry tonight," she said, closing the
menu. "I want one of everything!"

"Go ahead."

She laughed. "You'd have to roll me out of here."

"So what? At least you would have had a good
time."

The warmth and intensity in his eyes made her
breath catch. If only it had been like this when they
were married. If only they could have been friends
before they were lovers. "Thank you, Marco."

He set his menu aside. "And what have I done?"

Her hands lifted. "This," she said, gesturing to the night, the pretty lights, the festive atmosphere around them. "This is wonderful, Marco. This is really special. This time with you, with the girls, it helps more than you know."

"I think you're wonderful—"

"No."

"You are. You've an amazing attitude, Payton. You've a beautiful heart. And somehow you still manage to look sensational, too."

A knot formed in Payton's throat. When he complimented her, and looked at her with such warmth in his eyes, she felt fizzy on the insides. Felt ridiculously giddy and happy, almost like the night at the Trussardi's when he asked her to dance.

The night at the Trussardis had been just as magical. After dancing they'd gone outside to have a drink and they talked for an hour straight. When he offered her a ride home, she accepted without a second thought. It had never crossed her mind to seduce him. It hadn't crossed her mind that they'd even kiss.

But he did kiss her, he kissed her on her doorstep after he'd walked her to the entry of her pension. The small light above their heads attracted moths and the moths flit and flickered and Marco bent his head and covered her mouth with his and—magic

It hadn't been just a kiss, but *The Kiss*. The kiss of a lifetime. The kiss where everything in life made sense and emotion and intellect and passion came together for the first time ever.

Maybe the only time ever.

Even now she remembered how natural it had all

been, how uncomplicated it had felt. There had been no doubts, no questions. She just wanted more with him, more of his touch and more of his passion and more of the pleasure.

In his arms that one night she'd experienced something so powerful and so profound she'd never wanted anyone else. Couldn't contemplate being with anyone else.

"Payton."

Marco was saying her name, asking her a question. She jerked, returning to the present. "What was that?"

He smiled faintly. "I asked if you wanted more wine."

"No. I'm good. Thank you." She felt a bittersweet prick, a fluttering of regret. If only she and Marco had handled things differently, if only they'd been able to make the marriage work out.

The waiter presented them with the bill at the end of the meal. "Well, I'd consider dinner a success," Marco said, putting away his wallet.

"And we've done all right without our two little chaperones," Payton said.

"I'm not the one in need of a chaperone," he retorted.

Just what was he implying? "You think I need one?"

His eyes narrowed a little as his gaze settled on her mouth. "I think you want one."

It suddenly felt as if someone had let loose a hundred butterflies in her middle. "And why would I need one?"

His gaze left her mouth to slowly travel over her face. His intense scrutiny made her aware that her long hair had been tousled by the evening breeze and the scoop neck of her beaded camisole probably exposed more skin than it should.

"You think I'm immune to you?" he persisted, his deep voice dropping even lower. "You think I don't find you attractive anymore?"

"I don't know—"

"I do. For your information that mysterious spark which was there from the start has never gone away, never flickered out."

His words pulsed inside her, quickening her pulse, warming her body. She shouldn't get carried away. They were just words and yet she didn't know if it was the warm night or the wine she'd had with dinner, but she liked the way his words were making her feel. She liked the way his gaze made her belly knot and muscles tighten.

"This isn't smart, Marco."

"Have we ever been smart…at least when it came to each other?"

"But that's cause for alarm now, don't you think?"

"Maybe, maybe not. It all depends on one's perspective."

Perspective. Good word, she silently acknowledged, and something to think about right now. She needed to keep some perspective. If she lost her head, she wasn't the only one to get hurt.

There were the girls. And Marilena. That was at least three others impacted.

Payton forced herself to shut down her emotions,

deaden her senses. She had to act responsibly. She couldn't give in to hunger and need. "It's getting late. Maybe we should head back before Pietra starts worrying."

"Pietra's not going to worry. Besides, she'd love for us to stay out all night. She needs the cash."

"I should call her though." *Come on, keep your perspective. Put some distance between the two of you.* "I'll just go use the phone—"

"Here, use mine," he pleasantly interrupted, reaching into his coat pocket and holding the phone out.

His dark eyes met hers, challenging her and Payton felt a current of excitement fizz through her. He knew she didn't really want to call. He knew she was just trying to hang on to what was left of her self-control.

"Maybe later," she answered huskily.

He shrugged, a very Latin shrug, and slipped the tiny phone back into his pocket. "Just let me know."

And then he looked up at her again and the guard had dropped from his gaze, and in his eyes she saw heat, fire, hunger. He wanted her. He wanted to take her back to the house and strip her clothes off and do things she hadn't done in way too many years.

Then his mouth slowly curved into a sexy, sinful smile. "Don't get nervous."

"Who's nervous?"

"Payton, it's just you and me. We know each other well enough to let down our hair a little, have some fun together. You do still know how to have fun, don't you?"

Her heart raced. "Of course I do."

"Good." He was trying not to laugh at her. "Then

let's enjoy ourselves. The night's still young, you look unbelievably sexy, I think we ought to go dancing.''

They crossed the plaza and took a right on a side street, following the sound of thumping music. Payton spotted the disco by the long snaking line of bodies waiting outside the front door.

''I guess we can't dance after all,'' Payton said brightly, relieved that she wouldn't have to go shoulder to shoulder and hip to hip with Marco tonight. She didn't trust him in this mood.

''Not a problem,'' he answered, taking her hand.

He was right. There was no waiting in line and no charge for admission, either. The door manager spotted Marco and immediately waved him in. Nice life, Payton thought, as Marco led her through the disco's dark interior with the curving walls painted aquamarine-blue.

Marco found them a small booth on the side of the dance floor and whenever the shimmering disco ball turned and the strobe hit, the blue neon club turned ghostly white and silver. The music was loud and the bass thumped so hard the floor literally jumped.

Conversation was next to impossible and before Marco could order a bottle of wine, two cocktails arrived, the drinks the same shade of blue as the walls of the disco.

''Courtesy of the lady sitting at the booth over there,'' the cocktail waitress said, and she gestured to the booth on the other side of the disco. A young woman with a mass of golden-brown hair lifted her drink in salute.

Payton did a double-take. The "lady" was only America's biggest film star.

"You know Lyssa Harper?" Payton demanded, practically shouting to be heard over the music. She was trying not to stare but Lyssa was now blowing Marco kisses. The actress had either been drinking or had a major soft spot for Marco.

Marco shrugged. "I dressed her for this year's Oscars." He nodded at the drinks on the table. "Do you want this or should I order something a little more sedate?"

"Why should I want something more sedate?" She practically had to shout to be heard above the din.

He picked up the neon blue cocktail and took a sip. His nose wrinkled a little as he swallowed. "I just wasn't sure if you were ready for a Tongue in the Grotto."

She nearly choked on her own tongue. *"What?"*

"Tongue in the Grotto," he repeated, dark eyes glinting with amusement.

"I heard you. I just couldn't believe that's actually the drink's name."

"It's the house drink. Named after Capri's famous Grotta Azzurra. The Blue Grotto draws thousands of tourists each summer."

Tongue in the Grotto, indeed. She felt heat flood her cheeks and she crossed her legs, clenching her knees. "I don't think we've been there yet, have we?"

"No." Marco leaned toward her and whispered in her ear. "But it is something I've always wanted to do with you.'' And from his wicked expression she knew he didn't mean sightseeing, either.

Payton tried to drink the neon cocktail, but every time she lifted the bright blue vodka beverage to her mouth she pictured erotic activities that had nothing to do with touring a cave in a little four person rowboat.

''You can't drink it,'' Marco said watching her.

''It's a bit much for me. But that's fine. I don't really want anything else to drink.''

''Shall we dance then?''

It'd been years since they danced and yet it was something they both loved to do. Besides, it had to be safer than sitting and sipping potent cocktails with him. ''Please.''

He led her out onto the crowded dance floor and astonishingly the frenzied throng parted a little, giving them room.

They knew Marco, she realized. But then, most people here would. He was a regular on Capri. His family had been coming for three generations. His mother's father had even played a role in the island's colorful history.

The two fast songs gave way to a slow number and Marco drew her closer, his hand settling low on her waist, his thighs pressed against hers. She'd liked watching him dance—there was no question he knew how to move—but she enjoyed being in his arms even more. He had grace, strength, and the easy elegance of an athlete.

As they danced, Marco took her hand and lifted it to his mouth. His eyes met hers and turning her hand over, he kissed her wrist, his mouth so warm on the wild beating of her pulse. "I think this is exactly what you needed," he said. "What I needed, too."

Her wrist tingled and her heart pounded and she felt like they were on the start of a significant journey. Could they cross the great divide?

"I'm making you a promise, Payton. What you face, what you'll go through, you won't have to do it alone—"

"You don't have to do this."

"I know. But I want to. I'll be there with you. We'll do it together. No matter what happens, I'll be at your side."

Her eyes burned but she wasn't going to get weepy. The situation was complicated enough without her losing control of her emotions. "The princess is very generous, but I don't know that she'll appreciate your promise."

"It's not Marilena's choice. It's mine." He tugged her hand. "Don't look so stricken. Come, let's go outside. I think we could use some air."

She followed him across the crowded dance floor to the nearest door. He pushed the door open and they stepped outside into the considerably cooler night air. Overhead stars twinkled in a nearly black sky and Payton smelled the salt of the ocean.

"We need to talk about Marilena," he said abruptly. "I've wanted to talk to you about her, about us, for a while." He grimaced. "It seems as if there's an awful lot I've been wanting to discuss with you."

She crossed her arms over her chest, trying to adjust to the cooler temperature. "Maybe it's because we've never really talked. That night at the Trussardis's we seemed to have leap-frogged over a lot of steps.'' She swallowed. ''Like conversation.''

He shot her a swift glance, his expression a little mocking. ''Conversation didn't have the appeal of other activities.''

''Yes, and look at the problems appealing activities created.'' She didn't know where to laugh or cry. Their whole relationship had been such a disaster.

A waitress stepped outside to see if they needed anything and Marco ordered two bottles of mineral water. As the waitress disappeared Marco smiled. ''I didn't think we needed another blue drink.''

''Especially not if it has suggestive connotations.''

''Does it?'' he asked, feigning innocence. ''I thought it was paying homage to Capri's natural treasure.''

''Sure you did.''

He laughed quietly, the sound rumbling deep in his chest and leaned against the low stone wall with the ocean view. ''I've enjoyed myself tonight.''

She tipped her head back and looked up. The moon was nearly full and the stars were bright pricks of light against the inky blue black sky. It was a beautiful night. Marco had been great company. ''Me, too.''

They were silent for a moment listening to the disco's music pulse along with the crash of water on the rocks below. After a long moment Marco turned his head and looked at her. ''If we'd talked more, do you think we could have worked things out?''

CHAPTER TEN

PAYTON didn't know how he could make her heart ache with so few words. She turned a little, sat down on the edge of the wall. Even though she and Marco weren't touching she was so aware of him, so aware of everything that had happened between them. "I don't know. We probably would have still ended up separating, but it might have made the separation less painful."

He didn't speak for a long moment and they listened to. "I hate asking these questions, but I'm trying to understand. You make it sound like separation was inevitable with us. Why?"

She frowned as she tried to think of an appropriate answer. There were reasons, she knew there were lots of good reasons but at the moment she couldn't think of one. "I don't know. I just don't see how we could have worked our differences out."

"But why not? Fundamentally you're not bad. Fundamentally I'm not bad. In fact, we have quite a few things in common."

His persistence was making her feel a little crazy. What did he want her to say? What was the answer he was looking for?

She shifted against the wall, the rough stones and grout sharp against the back of her legs. "I'm really not much of a relationship expert. Dating wasn't considered an important part of my education.''

"But surely you had boyfriends.''

"Male friends, yes, but romantic relationships? Never. You were my first.''

"Lover.''

"First everything.'' She squirmed a little, feeling ridiculously gauche. "After seeing what my mom went through after my dad left, I tried to steer clear of relationships and I certainly never intended to get married.''

"But then I insisted on it.''

"You thought it'd be best for the girls.''

"It should have been. In an ideal world.''

Payton bit her lip, suppressing a sigh. His suggestion had made head sense, but their world wasn't an ideal world. Or perhaps hers hadn't been the ideal one. Marrying a man like Marco had simply overwhelmed her. It was like doing well in a local race and then being thrown into the Olympics. Marco was not an ordinary man, and life with Marco had been far from ordinary.

"You hated being married to me.'' He shot her an apprising glance. "In one argument I think I even called you on it.''

Heat flooded her cheeks. He was referring to a fight they'd had years ago just before he'd moved out of the Milan villa leaving her and the girls alone. "Your actual words were, 'ungrateful upstart American nobody'.''

"Ouch.'' He had the grace to wince. "Not very nice of me.''

She remembered the fight clearly, as well as the next nine miserable months. Months where she cried endlessly, missing him, missing their intimacy, missing everything she'd hoped for but had been denied. She'd loved him and yet hated the marriage. "And yes, I did hate being married to you. Less than a month after we married you moved out of the villa—" she broke off, a bubble of air trapped in her throat.

But now that she had time to think about it, she realized that Marco hadn't moved away. He hadn't cut off contact.

She'd been the one that couldn't handle seeing him after he left. She'd been the one filled with such pain and rage.

Had she subconsciously escalated the problems, turned a difficult situation into a full-blown war of the sexes? Worse yet, had she perhaps reenacted her parents' falling out?

"You were saying?" he prompted.

She shook her head. She didn't know how to share it, didn't know if she should.

The waitress returned with their bottles of mineral water and Marco paid her. But once the waitress disappeared back into the disco, Marco resumed their discussion.

"Why did you hate being married to me? It's what you wanted."

"What did I get being married to you? Certainly not your company!"

"You wanted my company?"

"Oh, Marco, what do you think?" Payton raised the bottle to her lips and taking a long cool drink.

"I thought you wanted the package."

"As in position, wealth, visibility?" She did laugh this time. "*Please.* I've never wanted a free ride, and quite frankly, I've never wanted anyone to provide for me. I can take care of myself."

"Which you were doing quite nicely these past two years."

"Until the diagnosis," she retorted, again aware of the grim reality that one had so little control in life.

They returned in silence to the villa and yet Payton's thoughts raced. She didn't know what to think, or feel. Part of her felt overwhelmed by all they'd discussed, and yet another part of her felt peace, as well as relief.

Pietra left and Marco locked up the house. At the door of her bedroom they said good-night.

He turned to leave and Payton stopped him, placing a hand on his sleeve. "Marco, during one of our fights before we divorced, you said I was only interested in the d'Angelo name and our conversation tonight reminded me of it."

"We said a lot of things back then—"

"I know." Her hand tightened on his forearm. "But it's important to me that you know this. I was fascinated by the d'Angelo name. I still am. But not for the reason you think. I could care less about the celebrity aspect. I'm intrigued by color, textiles, pattern. If I found you or your father interesting it's because I love what you do. What *we* do."

He still didn't get it, did he? Her attraction wasn't

based on his name, or even his handsome face. She was attracted to all of him. Attracted to his energy, his drive, his vision.

She loved him. It was that simple.

It was that complicated.

In his room Marco slowly stripped off his shirt, his pants, his silk boxers and showered in a spray of hot water, trying desperately to relax. His muscles felt bunched. His head throbbed with tension. Payton.

He still cared so much for her. It made him wonder what the hell he'd been thinking these past two years. Made him wonder what the hell he'd been doing.

He and Marilena were not right for each other and yet he'd spent years clinging to this ridiculous notion that she'd be the right wife, the right image, the right partner.

Why? What made Marilena the better choice than Payton? Marilena certainly didn't engage his emotions the way Payton did. With Marilena he always felt supremely in control. With Marilena he could suppress his emotions.

With Marilena he felt controlled. Rational. Reasonable.

With Payton he felt life intensely. He felt passionately. He felt, period.

He felt. Marco suddenly turned the shower off and stood in the marble shower enclosure, water dripping off him. He wiped a forearm across his face. Was that the problem? With Payton he felt emotions and the emotions scared him?

Grabbing his towel, Marco rubbed himself down

before pulling on a pair of comfortable Egyptian cotton pants he'd designed for lounge wear. The pants were cut from a Moroccan print the color of paprika. They hung low on his lean waist, exposing his hipbones and were comfortable for sleeping.

He used his fingers to comb his hair back from his brow and headed back to Payton's room.

She looked surprised to see him back at her bedroom door. "What's wrong?"

She'd showered, too, and in her black and white silk pajamas—men's style, he thought with a wry smile—she looked small and very young still. It suddenly occurred to him that she was still young. When they'd married she'd been just twenty-three. She'd soon be twenty-seven. He had almost twelve years on her—almost a lifetime of experience, not to mention wisdom. But had he ever acted wise? Had he acted mature?

Marco took in the tumble of dark red curls and the wide blue eyes and saw the innocence still there. He hadn't allowed himself to look at her closely in years. He hadn't want to acknowledge that he'd taken something from her that night when she'd lost her virginity. He hadn't wanted any emotional responsibility.

He'd hurt her. She'd been naive and he'd been ruthless. What a combination.

He couldn't change the past, but the future still lay ahead of them. "If you knew you only had four days left, what would you do?"

Her blue eyes widened, revealing flecks of purple and black in the blue irises. He'd shocked her with the question. "I'd spend as much time as possible with our girls."

He felt a vibration of emotion within him. "Is that it?"

"No." Her bottom lip caught between her teeth. "I'd want to spend as much time with you as I could, too."

He reached out and stroked her soft cheek. "I knew you'd say that."

"Am I that predictable?"

"No. It's what I hoped you say." Touching her, he felt a savage twist inside his chest, a wrench of emotion so strong it actually hurt. "Tell me, Payton. Is it too late to start over?"

She blinked, eyes growing moist. Her mouth trembled. "I thought we'd already agreed to work on becoming better friends."

There it was again, a reckless surge of hunger and adrenaline, a purely primitive response that made him want to take her and make her his. He didn't want to be just friends. He wanted more from her than friendship. He wanted some of the fire and hunger he'd tasted that first night. He'd made love to many women but making love with Payton had been more real, more intense than anything he'd ever felt before.

He cupped her cheek, savoring the warm satin texture of her skin even as he fought the animal impulse to devour her then and there. "You and I could never be just friends. There's too much here. Too much heat. Too much chemistry."

Payton swallowed hard, desperately trying to contain the chaotic emotions rising within her. His thumb was drawing slow circles against her cheek and she couldn't think, couldn't focus, not with his hand against her feverish cheek, and not with her whole body responding to his incredible touch.

God, she'd missed him. She'd missed being touched. Missed being loved by him. Yet touching him, kissing him, would only complicate things more. And hurt her more. Making love to Marco only heightened her emotions, made her love stronger, more powerful.

"It's late," she whispered faintly, knowing she had to pull away before she lost her head completely.

His mouth curved but his dark eyes didn't smile. He looked fierce. Determined. "It's not that late."

She reached up to clasp his hand, wanting to lift it from her cheek. Instead she found herself holding him, holding on as if terrified to let go.

But this is just what she couldn't let happen. She couldn't start wanting and needing. She couldn't become vulnerable again.

Fight it, Payton. Fight back. If you don't resist now, you never will.

Unshed tears thickened in her throat, burning the back of her eyes. "I think I hear the girls."

"I don't hear anything."

"You don't know what to listen for," she answered, her heart hammering harder as his palm slipped, his hand flush against neck, his thumb against the base of her throat as if taking her pulse.

He wasn't about to be distracted. "And what if they did come? They wouldn't see anything but me touching you."

"But Marilena—"

"Isn't here, and she isn't part of the equation." His head dipped, his mouth brushed her cheek. The caress felt as if he'd set her face on fire. "The equation is Marco, Payton, Gia and Liv. The four of us. That's all that should matter to you."

She trembled as he caressed her neck and throat. Her sensitivity to him was overwhelming. It had been like this that very first night, it'd been raw and intense and she, completely inexperienced, had just let it happen.

But she was older now and more experienced. She knew better. She couldn't switch off her brain—much less her conscience. Marco might be able to forget Marilena tonight, but she couldn't. Yes, she craved him, absolutely craved his mouth and his hands and his touch, she also knew that this, being together, was wrong.

"No, no, no," she whispered, hands against his chest, her fingers spread to push him away. "I can't do this, Marco. You're not mine—"

"I'm not anyone's," he answered thickly. "I belong to no one."

"But Marilena!"

His dark head lifted, his eyes blazed. "It's over between us."

Payton felt a spike of elation immediately followed by guilt. She loved Marco, still wanted to be with Marco, but to take him from another woman?

"This is my choice," he said almost fiercely. "I don't love her, not the way I should."

"You're saying that now, but it's the heat of the moment. What if you change your mind later?"

"Heat of the moment, is it?" Marco demanded as he reached into his pocket and held up a gold band with an enormous stone. "Then what is this?"

Payton stared at the marquis-cut diamond for the longest time. "Whose is that?"

"You know perfectly well."

"Marco—"

"You didn't believe me when I said I'd ended it with Marilena. Well, here is your proof. Her ring. What more do you want?"

Payton's eyes searched his. She felt such horribly conflicting emotions. Hope and fear. Excitement and guilt. Her gaze dropped to the ring in his hand. The enormous stone glinted in the light.

"You said if you only had four days left, you'd want to spend as much time with me as possible." Marco tilted her chin up, forcing her eyes to meet his again. "I feel the same way about you. If you're the one I want to be with, and you're the one I want to raise my children, how can I be with her? How can I consider marrying her?"

"But you said once you had much in common. You said you had a similar background and shared values—"

"I also thought I'd lost you forever. I thought you were never coming back, and God forgive me for saying this, but Marilena was an expensive insurance policy. My relationship with her kept me from being hurt by anyone again."

"You lose her, you lose that policy," Payton whispered.

"I know. But that policy wasn't working anyway. You came back and you brought me news that you're sick, and could possibly die, and I realize I'm nothing but a fool. I've been playing safe for years and playing safe is just stupid. It's a coward's way out and I may be a lot of things, but I'm not a coward. And I'd rather have four days with you than a lifetime with another woman."

He closed the bedroom door and moved toward her. "I feel like the clock is ticking, Payton. Haven't we talked enough for one night?"

She knew he was going to kiss her and she wanted the kiss as much as she feared it. She knew that when they touched reason when out the window.

Hands on her upper arms, he pulled her against him. His head lowered, his mouth descended, covering hers. She could feel his own ambivalence, feel his frustration the tension of his arms and the hard press of his mouth. At one level he wanted to punish her, wanted her to feel the pain he'd felt, but even as his lips crushed hers, his arms gentled, his hands leaving her upper arms to cradle her head.

He shifted slightly, adjusting her against him and the anger was gone, leaving only his warmth, his impatience, his strength. She felt the tight corded muscles of his thighs and the relentless pressure of his hips. He wanted her, that much she knew, and when his lips parted hers, she shivered, overwhelmed by her own longing.

Marco took a step into her, parting her thighs to

bring them even closer and the rub of his aroused body against her own made every nerve ending scream.

But she couldn't think, couldn't think straight at all with his hands on her and his body touching hers and the scorching heat all around. Part of her brain still ordered her to pull away while another part overrode her protest, desperate for warmth—even more desperate for long denied gratification.

Her craving for contact won.

With a sigh she slid her hands across Marco's chest, her body melting into his. Marco clasped her hips and pulled her forward, bringing her hips square against his. The sinewy pressure of his body was sinful. Payton shuddered as his warmth penetrated her silky pajama top and the thin silk pants, his hard contours familiar and yet shocking.

Marco shifted and lifting her arms, Payton wrapped them around his neck. She'd always been attracted to him but the desire had never been so physical, or intense. Her breasts ached, her blood raced, her lower belly practically pulsed and she pressed herself against him to satisfy the craving.

"God help me, but I want you even more now than before," Marco muttered, drinking her in, drawing her as close as he could.

The waistband on his pajamas rubbed at her and he ran a hand down the length of her torso, his fingers tracing the ridge of bone in her hip before cupping her tummy.

Payton felt mindless, nerveless. She's ignored her body for years but now it refused to be denied. She wanted Marco. She wanted Marco to touch her. She wanted to touch him, all of him. She wanted to be with him once more. Who knew what would happen when she returned to San Francisco. The future was dark, cloudy, impossible to read. All she had was the moment. All she had was right now.

And right now she wanted another kiss. Another caress…

She fit herself against him, blind to anything but the delicious feel of his arms and mouth. That night after the opera, the night they lost control, it had been potent, powerful, but nothing like this. This hunger felt hot and hard and razor sharp. This hunger was a tangible thing.

Marco's lips parted hers and Payton welcomed the rasp of his tongue and its hard thrust inside her mouth. His tongue teased hers. She answered its quest. Blood throbbed in her lips, echoing the heavy pulse in her belly.

Clasping her hip, Marco pressed her against his arousal. Payton gasped, her body tightening, instinct overriding coherent thought. She could feel him in every nerve of her body.

"I want you," he said, his breathing deep, hoarse.

"Yes." She looked up at him, her brain slow, thoughts fuzzy. A lock of black hair fell across his forehead. Emotion glowed in his dark eyes.

He swallowed hard and touched her cheek. "We have to be careful."

"Yes." What had happened to her brain? It felt like scrambled eggs.

"Are you on anything for birth control?"

She exhaled and shook her head, her limbs trembling. God, she wanted him. She wanted to strip here and now and feel him inside her, feel his skin against hers, feel the warmth and energy and excitement. "No. Don't you have a—" She gestured to his pocket. "A condom?"

"I don't carry condoms in my wallet, and I haven't anything here at the house." He must have read her troubled expression. "Marilena and I weren't kids. We didn't make out in parked cars or in dark corners."

His head dipped. He kissed the edge of her mouth, his lips sending fire throughout her middle all over again.

She swayed on her feet and reached up to clasp his shirt, trying to steady herself. "We can still make love," she whispered. "We'll just be careful. Just pull out before."

He shook his head, the dark shock of hair on his brow making him look rakish, wild. "It's too risky. We only made love once before—"

"It wasn't once. We made love three times that night."

His eyes glinted. "Yes, but it was just one night and all it took was one night with you and we conceived twins. We can't take risks like that now, not with you facing chemo when you go home."

He caught her face in his hands, lifted her face to his. "But just because I can't be inside you doesn't mean we can't make love in other ways."

CHAPTER ELEVEN

THE inflection in his voice thrilled her and she gripped his shirt even tighter, needing to hold on for support. Beneath his shirt she felt the strong planes of his chest, his muscle dense and smooth.

One of Marco's hands trailed beneath the waistband of her silk pajama pants, tracing an invisible line across her tense belly.

It felt as if he'd torched her, white and blue and gold flames licking at her skin, melting her on the inside. Her body ached with emptiness, her legs quivered as he pushed her silky pajama pants down to her ankles before stripping them off each ankle.

She was standing there in tiny lace panties and an oversized pajama shirt and yet she didn't have a scrap of modesty left, her senses too heightened, her body too hot with wanting.

His fingertips caressed down a bare thigh and back up the inside. He was spreading the fire everywhere. Her mouth parted and dried as he stroked over her lace panty before his palm cupped her mound.

Mercy, she panted, have mercy on me. His fingers moved beneath the silk-trimmed panty and lightly caressed her, lightly running across the outer shape of her and Payton wanted to scream. It was exciting and yet completely unsatisfying. To have his hand so close to everything without really doing anything was as close to torture as Payton wanted to come.

"What's wrong?" Marco's lips brushed her cheek and then the curve of her ear. "You seem a little tense."

"Don't be mean."

He lightly stroked her again, but again it was across her and very general. The pleasure was general and what one wanted when there, so close to hot points, was specifics.

She hauled herself against him, her camisole too tight across her breasts, the tiny beading grating her taut nipples. "More would be nice," she managed, feeling carnal and hedonistic and not giving much of a damn anymore.

"How?"

She blushed. He knew perfectly well how. He'd done it before, he was very good with his hands, had quite the expert touch if she remembered correctly. "Touch *me*."

"I am touching you."

She could have sworn he was laughing a little. How unfair was that? "This isn't the time," she said, heat surging to her cheeks, making her feel impossibly hot. "There is a time to tease but it's not now."

Her head had tipped back giving him access to her neck and his lips slowly traveled across her skin, lighting silver sparklers as he went. "So tell me what you want. How should I be touching you?"

And then he did it. He slid a finger between her inner lips, stroked across the sensitized nerve before entering her.

Her legs nearly went out and she shuddered. The touch was intimate and yet exquisite. There were times she felt like a body, like pure energy in motion, and then there was now when she felt incredibly sexual and feminine. Marco knew how to make her feel like a woman. He was the only one who'd ever made her feel this way and it was intense. It was so delicious and addictive that she could almost imagine becoming a slave to desire. A slave to skin and passion.

He pushed into her, his fingers warm and slick. Payton's legs wobbled, her ankles almost floppy in the high heels.

"I don't think I can stand," she choked as he caressed her deeper.

"Fine. You can sit." He shifted and then lifting her up, placed her on the edge of her small elegant writing desk. "This is a better position for me anyway," he added, parting his knees and crouching in front of her.

She sucked in a hoarse breath as she felt the tip of his tongue flick over her hot sensitive flesh and she had a very vivid picture of the famous Capri cocktail. One way or another, she thought, panting a little at the intense sensation, Marco had been determined she try the exotic, erotic Tongue in the Grotto.

With his mouth he brought her to the pinnacle of pleasure, and her body quivered with such violent aftershocks she couldn't move from the desk for quite some time, holding tightly on to Marco instead.

"I feel like Mount Vesuvius erupting," she choked with embarrassed laughter against his neck. She'd never had such an intense sensual experience before.

He laughed, too, and swung her into his arms. ''I think bed's the place for you. It has to be more comfortable than your writing desk.''

Under the covers, she curled against him, her hand stroking his hard flat abdomen. She felt the muscles in his belly tighten at her light touch and as she stroked lower she heard his sharp inhale.

There were so many things they'd never done together and suddenly Payton wanted to try all of them. Marco had been wonderful giving her pleasure, now she wanted to do the same for him. But before she made any obvious move, she contented herself with just touching him, wrapped her hand around the rigid length of him and slowly but firmly stroking. From the sound of it, she'd found the right tempo but Payton wasn't about to let him come too soon.

Sliding down his chest, she let her breasts tickle and tease until she'd disappeared beneath the covers. She used her mouth to discover him, the tip of her tongue to trace him.

His muffled groan of pleasure aroused her. She'd loved the way he touched her, and yet it was almost more gratifying being able to return the pleasure. Making love was powerful, and as she stroked him with her hand and mouth she felt a welling of love, perhaps appreciating for the first time the differences between them. If he weren't Marco, and she weren't Payton, none of this would be half as wonderful.

She loved Marco. She did with all her heart.

The next morning after breakfast Marco announced he had something special planned. He immediately had the twins attention. "I thought we'd go visit a special place," he said. "We leave in a couple days but you can't leave until you've seen the Grotta Azzurra."

The Blue Grotto. Payton's cheeks warmed, remembering the explicit lovemaking from the night before. She knew she'd never hear the name of Capri's famous cavern without thinking something entirely different.

Although most people didn't bother with life jackets, Marco insisted the twins wear them as they transferred from the motor launch into the tiny rowboat.

Payton had expected that the hype around the caves would be just that, but as the oarsmen rowed them through the mouth of the cave they were immediately circled by intense blue light, the blue light coming from beneath the water and glowing with a supernatural luminosity.

It was unlike anything she'd ever seen before. The neon-blue took her breath away.

No one spoke in the cave. The quiet was like that of a great Gothic cathedral, no one felt like breaking the serene stillness.

But back on the dock the girls couldn't stop talking about the blueness of the water and the strange blue light. "Like from outer space," Gia said, eyes big, hands flying. She talked like a true Italian, all passionate gestures and energy.

It was noon when they finished their excursion and Marco suggested they stop for lunch at the popular and always crowded Piazzetta for pizza and Italian sodas. Despite the crowds, they were seated immediately—it seemed to be Marco's good fortune to never wait in line—and they ate outside under a bright blue and white striped awning.

On their way back to the villa, Marco mentioned he had one quick errand to do and asked the taxi driver to pull over at a small convenience store. It wasn't until they were home that Marco showed Payton his purchase. He opened the paper bag and she peeked in.

Condoms. Dozens of them. ''You're not taking a chance, are you?'' she mocked.

''No. Because last night was good, but it wasn't enough. I want to be inside you.''

The moment the girls were tucked in for the night, Marco picked up a bottle of wine, two glasses, and led Payton to the bedroom.

There were few preliminaries and no more discussion. Payton felt Marco's urgency as he kissed her, undressed her, his hands cupping her breasts before caressing her hips, and the curve of her bottom.

''I've thought of nothing all day but being with you, touching you.'' His voice sounded hoarse and he dipped his head to suckle her breast. With her nipple in his mouth, he slowly circled the rosy aureole with his tongue, drawing smaller and smaller circles until he concentrated on just the aching nipple.

Payton buried her face against his shoulder, her lips parting in a helpless moan. She loved the way he touched her, loved the wild sensation flooding her veins, but it didn't answer the emptiness her.

''How can I want you like this?'' she choked, her voice breathless, hoarse.

"Because you know I want you just as much, if not even more."

When Marco finally entered her, and his body filled her, they were fierce, their movements wild, even a little desperate. They hit the peak fast and yet they both still wanted more.

"I'd never get tired of this," Payton sighed as she rested her cheek on Marco's chest. "Nothing in the world feels like this."

"I agree. This is good. Better than good, this is amazing."

The next three days passed as more of the same. Swimming and playing with the girls during the day and then spending half the night making love. It was as if they were learning about each other for the first time, learning that they had more in common than twin daughters and a shared passion for design.

They loved to tease each other and enjoyed endless contact. They'd bump into each other during the day just to feel pressure and skin. They'd touch beneath the table. Walk holding hands.

Payton felt like she was a newlywed finally getting her honeymoon.

On their last night in Capri, they stayed up late, enjoying the warm air, the beautiful moon, the reflection of light against the water.

When they turned in, they went to Marco's room and silently they stripped off their clothes and very silently made love. It was their last night on the island and the moment felt poignant, charged with meaning.

Making love was also different. They'd found a

new comfort with each other. Their bodies instinctively responded. They knew what each other liked and needed.

Marco intentionally kept Payton from peaking too soon, changing the tempo to delay her release. He didn't want the night to end. He didn't want to lose any of the intimacy or happiness he'd known during the past week.

But Marco could only hold back so long and he built the rhythm again, allowing the pleasure to build. He could feel himself near the edge and as he drove into Payton with deep hard thrusts he felt her tighten around him, felt her hands clench his arms and he covered her mouth with his, drinking her cry of ecstasy into him.

If only it could always be this way, he thought later. If only there were more moments like this, moments where he felt utter peace.

"You're too good," Payton murmured huskily, running a hand through his hair, ruffling the weight of it.

She was still so warm and lightly damp. He loved the feel of her, the shape of her, the smell of her. She was so real, and natural and gorgeous.

"*Bella,*" he murmured, kissing her. "*Mia bella Amore.*"

Then he shifted her, rolling her onto her back so he could look into her face. "This has been nice, yes?"

"Heavenly." She smiled and traced a line in his face, one of the grooves that paralleled his mouth.

"You've given me five amazing days and five perfect nights. I've never felt so content."

He felt the same. "I told you Capri was magical."

"You were right. When we arrived here I was so nervous, so afraid of everything." Her fingers were gentle as they explored his face. "I don't feel that way anymore. I feel brave. I'm afraid of nothing."

His chest hurt. She might not be afraid, but he was. He couldn't bear to think he still might lose her after everything they'd been through. "Marry me."

She blinked. She didn't say anything. She just stared up at him.

"Marry me and stay in Milan," he continued. "There's no reason not to. It's right for the children and it's the right thing for us. You need me with you in the coming months, and Payton, *bella*, I need to be with you."

"Marco, we've tried this before."

"So?" He pushed the sheet away, and lowered himself slowly over her, his weight supported by his arms.

She reached up to press against his chest. "It didn't work, remember?"

His knee separated her thighs, parting her legs to make room for him. "It didn't work because we weren't being mature. But we're older. We know better. We know that the girls' happiness is the most important thing, and the girls will need us together now more than ever before."

As his body lowered, and his mouth covered hers, Payton felt a wave of intense emotion. Once upon a time she'd had a dream. It had been to come to Italy, to see the great art and cathedrals of ancient Rome…

Marco entered her and Payton nearly cried out loud with hunger, with pleasure.

"Besides," he added, burying himself in her, filling her completely, "this time we have love on our side."

The next morning they were took a helicopter from Anacapri to the Naples airport, and then a private plane from Naples to Milan.

The air in Milan felt hot and heavy after the bliss of Capri. Marco's driver unloaded their luggage at Marco's ornate villa on the outskirts of the city.

The girls immediately trotted off to go play and Marco captured Payton's hand as they stood in the entry.

"You haven't given me an answer," he said, his deep voice pitched low.

Payton felt his tension, his leashed passion and as his dark eyes held hers, she felt herself fall, falling hard, falling for him all over again.

Being with Marco was like a fantasy, but better because it was real. *He* was real. His kindness and strength weren't illusions. When her health was jeopardized, he stepped forward and he went to work making everything all right for all of them.

Her heart turned over as he lowered his head and kissed her gently. "Marry me, Payton."

"Marco—"

"I don't want to hear no. I don't want a maybe. Say yes, Marco, I'll marry you. Say yes, Marco, I'll marry you this weekend."

And God help her, the word no wasn't in her vocabulary, at least when it came to Marco d'Angelo. Wrapping her arms around his neck Payton's lips softened beneath his, and she gave him her heart as she kissed him. "Yes, Marco. I'll marry you this weekend."

They couldn't do another big wedding, nor did they want another big wedding. Marco suggested they have a very small private ceremony in the chapel of the beautiful Santa Maria del Carmine, a seven-hundred-year-old church not far from Marco's showroom. The ceremony was so private, in fact, that Marco invited no one outside the immediate family. Gia and Livia would be the only witnesses and Payton was pleased. She wanted the emphasis on the vows, not on frills and fuss.

The morning of the ceremony Marco knocked on Payton's bedroom door—he'd insisted on keeping her own room at the villa until they were legally married—and Payton answered dressed in only a white silk robe.

"I have something for you," Marco said, leaning against the door.

Payton looked at his black tuxedo and white tie. "You're wearing black tie! I thought we were going informal."

"No."

"But it's just a private ceremony. I thought it was just us."

"Yes, but it's still special." His dark eyes met hers. "Especially for me. I'm so glad we have a chance to do this over again. I'm so glad we have a chance to get this right.''

A lump filled her throat. ''Me, too.'' She blinked, refusing to get weepy today, even if it was her wedding day. ''I just wish I had something more appropriate to wear. You look gorgeous, Marco. You look like a model.''

''I'm sure you have something elegant in your closet. You're a fashion maven, Payton.'' He leaned forward, kissed her, caressing the length of her neck. ''Remember, you're Calvanti's future.''

He was teasing her and she laughed. The warmth in his voice more than made up for her disappointment in not having anything spectacular to wear to the church today. ''You said you had something for me?''

''How does a prenuptial sound?''

Her heart did a nosedive and she stared at him. ''Horrible,'' she said flatly. ''Especially last minute.''

He laughed at her irate expression. ''Good, because I don't have one. But there is something in your closet, at the back. In the zipper hanging bag.''

Payton rummaged through the closed and found the large garment bag. It was the kind of bag which designers used for couture gowns. ''What is this?''

''What do you think?

''A dress.''

''Good girl. You've always been very clever.''

Her eyes burned and she furiously blinked, wondering how on earth he could make her cry by giving her a dress. She made dresses for a living. It's what she did full-time. Yet to have a dress from Marco felt intimate—special. He'd never designed anything for her before.

She lay the garment bag on her bed and with shaking hands undid the zipper.

The gown's bodice was a snug white boned corset beaded with countless pearls. The skirt was white and full, a frothy silk organza and as she slid the dress from the bag, the white frothy silk gave way to a pumpkin and flame underskirt.

"You look beautiful in white, but fire suits you."

Marco's quiet voice was too much on top of everything and hugging the dress, Payton started to cry. "No one's made me a dress since I was a little girl." She couldn't stop the tears and she couldn't let them fall on the dress. "This is exquisite. This is absolutely lovely."

He approached her, wiped the tears from beneath her eyes. "I designed it in Capri. I've had seamstresses working on it night and day for nearly a week."

"But I only said yes yesterday!"

"I wasn't going to give up," he answered. "I was going to keep asking until you said yes."

In the soft glow of candlelight Marco and Payton said their vows and exchanged rings in Santa Maria's domed chapel with the soft wash of color from the old frescoes overhead. Late-afternoon sunlight spilled through the stained-glass windows, painting the walls like living jewels and illuminating the girls white pinafores and ruby colored sashes.

The girls were beautiful but no one glowed brighter than Payton, Marco thought, as the late-afternoon sun haloed her head, and shimmered off her gown. The snug boned corset revealed her elegant shoulders and creamy skin and her long red hair was softly looped back in loose ringlets. The white organza over flame silk was the perfect foil for Payton's personality. Sweetness and spice. Delicate and fierce.

His chest ached and he felt a rush of emotion so strong that it took him by surprise. To think he'd allowed his pride to keep them apart! It was unfathomable.

The brief ceremony over, they headed out for a private party, one nearly as intimate as the wedding. Marco had reserved a table at an exclusive restaurant in the city center and by the time they arrived, their dozen guests were waiting.

The guests were all friends and colleagues of Marco's—mainly designers, photographers, artists— and they welcomed Marco and Payton's appearance with shouts of approval.

The twins were only scheduled to stay for the first hour of dinner before Pietra would take them back to the villa. In the meantime they enjoyed the attention as Marco carried them and everyone offered congratulations and kisses for Payton and the girls.

The celebratory toasts started almost right away, with glasses of champagne lifted not just once, but dozens of times, and each toast became a little longer, a little more ebullient.

Marco caught her eyes as another toast ended and he smiled at her. His high Latin cheekbones glowed in the golden candlelight and Payton thought he looked supremely satisfied. It didn't hurt that his tuxedo—which was also his design—fit him like a glove. Some men wore tuxedos as if they were uncomfortable suits of armor, but Marco's black jacket clung to his broad shoulders and outlined the hard planes of his chest.

As the evening grew late, Marco returned yet again to Payton's side. His dark gaze studied her intently. ''Regrets?''

She laughed and stood on tiptoe to kiss him. ''Not one.''

CHAPTER TWELVE

WITH Pietra staying at the villa with the girls, Marco and Payton spent their wedding night at the Four Seasons, Milan's most exclusive hotel. A former monastery before being transformed into a hotel, the luxurious Four Seasons was situated in the heart of the fashion district just a stone's throw from Marco's headquarters.

Marco could hardly wait to get Payton inside their room before stripping off her gown and carrying her to bed in nothing but her lace garter belt and silk stockings.

Their lovemaking was hot and torrid and they'd barely caught their breath when a knock sounded at their door. "Housekeeping," a voice called through the door.

Still floating in that lovely afterglow, Payton turned to look at Marco. "I thought you put a do not disturb sign on the door."

"I did." He sat up, leaning on one elbow. "We're fine," he shouted toward the door. "We don't need anything."

There was a moment of silence and then paper rustled. A large manila envelope appeared beneath the door. Marco swore, exasperated. "*Incredible!* Does no one listen around here?"

"Don't worry. Stay there. I'll get it." Wearing

166

nothing but the white lace garter belt Payton left the bed.

''It's for you,'' she said, returning to the middle of the rumpled bed.

She handed Marco the envelope and sat down next to him, her dark red hair tumbling across her pale, damp skin.

But Marco wasn't interested in mail. A naked Payton with flushed cheeks, swollen lips and a white lace garter belt were too tempting to ignore.

Dropping the envelope on the ground, he wrapped an arm around Payton, his fingers sliding beneath the lace garter belt to play her skin. She gasped as he bent his head and covered one rosy-tipped nipple with his warm wet mouth.

She gasped again at the flick of his tongue. He sucked her nipple, rubbing the tight bud between his teeth. Payton felt a surge of hunger and her hips rocked, helplessly rotating.

Whimpering, she clasped his head with her hands and held him firmly to her breast. Her body felt so hot she thought she'd pop out of her skin.

He was turning her on again, making her want more, and she shifted, wiggling closer to him needing to feel the hard contours of his body against her.

They made love yet again, even more slowly than before, prolonging the pleasure of release until neither could stand it a moment longer.

Afterwards they slept, and Payton stirred, dreamily wakened by a hand—and mouth—doing the most amazing things to her. When she realized that the pleasure was no dream, rather it was Marco and he was already quite hungry for so early in the morning she tried to slip away.

"You can't do that," she protested, a little shocked even as she was very aroused.

"Watch me," he answered as he pulled the covers back over his head and proceeded to ravish her with very expert hands and a talented tongue.

It seemed like hours later when Payton stepped into the shower and let the hot water stream down. Before reaching for a bottle of shampoo, she tipped her head back, feeling the water pulse on her scalp, drenching her hair.

Her body hummed and throbbed.

Marco had loved her quite thoroughly. She still felt his size and length, felt the imprint of his hands everywhere. After hours of uninhibited lovemaking, she was definitely satiated, and a little bit sore.

She'd never imagined enjoying doing the things she did with Marco, and yet with him, everything felt right. Everything felt natural.

Payton was just stepping from the glass shower, securing an enormous towel around her middle, when Marco called her name. It was hard to hear him over the fan in the bathroom and she wrapped her wet hair in a second towel before opening the door. "Yes?"

She'd thought perhaps room service had arrived with coffee and hot rolls but there was no tray, or trolley. Instead Marco stood there staring at the sheet of paper in his hand.

"What the hell is going on?" he demanded.

She adjusted the turbanlike towel on her head and switched off the fan. "What did you say?"

Marco lifted his head, gazed at Payton who looked as if she'd been swallowed alive by two feuding bath towels and felt as if he'd throw up.

It couldn't be.

She wouldn't hide something this important from him. She wouldn't keep something like this a secret.

He nearly gagged, his mouth tasted bitter, a little cold and metallic. The past returned to him in a sharp flash, his brain suddenly clear—too clear—and he saw it all again: the shock of her pregnancy, the announcement to his Marilena, the sudden, swift change in focus and direction.

He'd never forget the moment he realized his life wasn't his life anymore. He'd never forget that she'd forced his hand.

His choices had been limited. There were fewer options.

She'd tricked then. She'd tricked him again.

"Marco, you look ill."

She was moving toward him, bare feet padding across the floor, her expression so damn innocent it made his chest burn. "I feel ill," he said.

"Is it your stomach? Did you eat something?"

"No."

"Take something?"

He suddenly pictured her as she'd been late last night, straddling his hips. Her long red hair streaming like fire past smooth shoulders and milky white skin.

He remembered how he tugged at the lace garter around her slim waist, dragging it down across her smooth flat belly and rounded hips.

He remembered the way she smelled when she

leaned forward to kiss him, her curls brushing his chest, sliding across his nipple. She'd smelled of love and sex and spice. She'd been wearing his new perfume, the one she'd helped with the ad, and the fragrance on her flushed skin, the scent of her body, the sway of her breasts as her lips covered his—

Seductress. Temptress. *Con artist.*

"Marco. Say something. What's wrong?"

He felt like someone had died. He felt like he'd been given tragic news. This couldn't be...this couldn't be happening again.

"Marco."

"There were no malignant cells."

"What?"

The goddamn innocence. It was an act, all an act. Again.

He ground his jaw tight, ground his teeth on a bitterness that he could taste. "The biopsy is clean. The results are negative. Both results are negative. You're fine."

She moved toward him, hands out as if to embrace him. "My God, Marco, that's wonderful! Can it possibly be true?"

"You tell me, Payton. You're the actress." Marco's cold voice practically sliced through her.

Payton had stopped walking. Her body went numb. "What are you saying?"

"I'm saying you've known about this all along, that you got the news just before we went to Capri and you kept it from me."

"No."

"You knew before we got married you were healthy. Admit it."

"I can't admit something I didn't do!" Payton's heart raced and yet her limbs felt icy. She didn't understand this, didn't understand any of this. Her brain raced but her thoughts were going in circles. She couldn't seem to see her way clear to the truth. "What was in the envelope?"

"Your lab reports."

"May I please see them?"

He laughed bitterly. "Why? You already know what they say. *Laboratory error, human mistake.*" His short brutal words danced along her head. "It wasn't even your film the lab was reading."

Payton's legs nearly gave way. "It was all a fluke?"

"Yes, *cara*. All one big miserable mistake." He turned around and walked out of the bathroom. He was reaching for his clothes, pulling on boxers and slacks, before doing the zipper.

Payton was dressing just as fast. "Where are you going, Marco?"

"I don't know. I just have to get out of here."

"Marco, you have to believe that I had no idea. I never was told—"

"Bullshit." He turned around and grabbed the paperwork off the bed. "Look at this. Read it. Phone call made to Payton Smith d'Angelo, May 31. Second phone call made, June 1 patient requests hard copy of paperwork—"

"But I didn't."

"Third notation," he continued, ignoring her protest. "Documentation express mailed to *Milan* and signed for." He looked up at her, his dark eyes burning. "What is it you want from me, Payton? Why do you have to play these games?"

She couldn't answer him. Couldn't think of a single thing to say. He didn't believe her, wasn't even listening to her. How could he love her if there was no trust?

She watched as he pulled his knit shirt over his head and slipped his feet into shoes.

If he left now she knew it would never be the same. He'd shatter her heart all over again. "Please, Marco, stay. Please don't leave me, not like this."

He heard the sob in his voice but it didn't move him, didn't touch him. At the moment he was numb. He could fee nothing.

"Don't let her do this," Payton begged, chasing him to the door.

Marco froze, his hand glued to the door knob. *"Her?"*

"Her, him, whoever it was," she answered emotionally, close to losing control. "Who would do this anyway? Who would do this on our wedding night? Think about it, Marco, someone doesn't want us together and this person is determined to hurt you. Hurt *us.*"

He knew in the back of his mind she had a point. He knew that someone had collected this information and put it inside an envelope and addressed it to him, here, at their bridal suite at the hotel but the act didn't change the facts. Payton had never been honest with him, never forthright.

He felt sick at heart, incredibly confused. Last night had been the happiest of his life. But this…? What in hell was going on?

Payton was either cruel or crazy, and she obviously needed help. How could she do this to him? To the girls? To all of them? Cancer wasn't a joke. He remembered all their discussions, the conversation about chemo, the appointment to cut her hair…he shuddered, appalled and sickened all over again.

What sane woman would put her family through this? What sane woman would drag her children—and her husband—to hell and back?

"Please, Marco." Payton's voice shook. She was still struggling to get her shoes on. "Let me come with you. We can talk. We can work this out—"

"I don't want to work things out." All he knew was that he had to get away from her. He couldn't bear to be in the same room with her, couldn't bear to look at her, listen to her.

Payton watched Marco leave and she stopped dressing, her hand going to her stomach. Her black satin blouse puckered beneath her hand and she felt skin. What had just happened?

How had the most perfect day of her life turn into the worst nightmare?

Payton didn't know what to do. They'd planned to spend the weekend at the hotel. It was a short honeymoon but after their week in Capri Payton knew Marco needed to get back to work, and she had been eager to meet with a specialist here in Milan.

Payton picked up the official looking letter lying on the bed. The letterhead was dark blue, raised ink and from the medical director at the oncology lab in San Francisco.

She read through the letter and there was lots of mumbo jumbo in it, and lots of excuses but the important thing to know was that she wasn't ill, her biopsy had come back clean. Unfortunately a lab assistant had inadvertently switched her film with someone else's.

Payton looked up, the letter settling into her lap. So someone else had cancer. Just not her.

This should have been wonderful news. This should have been cause for celebrating.

But there was no celebrating. Marco had gone and their wedding night had been poisoned.

It was early Sunday morning. Marco didn't know where to go. They were supposed to stay at the hotel through the weekend and Pietra would be with the girls at the house right now. He could go home, but he didn't think he could handle seeing the girls right now. The girls reminded him of Payton. He couldn't bear to even think about Payton.

Why would she do this? Once she found out the diagnosis was a mistake, why didn't she tell him? Why did she continue with the charade?

His confusion gave way to fresh rage. He didn't need this. He was tired, under pressure at work, overwhelmed by the demands of running a huge business.

There was no way he'd let her get away with this. He wasn't going to be tricked into marriage a second time. He'd divorce her so fast she wouldn't know what hit her. In fact, he'd serve her with papers and file for custody.

Sole custody.

He'd keep the girls. He'd get a court order and he'd keep the girls. Payton could do whatever the hell she liked—head back to California, get an apartment in Milan, move to Tahiti—he didn't care anymore. But regardless of what she did, he'd keep the girls and he'd damn well protect them from her.

Once driving Marco couldn't stop. Driving was the only way he could keep himself occupied and keep his temper in check. He got on the autostrada and never got off until he hit the lakes region, and then he pulled off the highway at Lake Como, refilled his gas tank and had dinner.

After dinner he began the drive back to Milan and he reached the villa just before midnight. He was tired from hours at the wheel and lack of sleep. He and Payton hadn't slept much the night before. They'd been too busy making love.

Parking in his garage, he climbed the stairs into the darkened villa. Pietra appeared in the hallway. *"Ciao,"* she sleepily greeted.

He nodded grimly.

She pushed hair from her eyes. "Everything all right?"

Marco was tempted to lie and then realized he didn't have the energy. *"Non bene."* Not good.

Pietra looked worried. "Do you want me to stay tonight?"

"Per favore. Grazie." He hesitated at the foot of

the stairs. "Payton—" he broke off, finding it almost impossible to say her name. "Has she been here?"

"*No.*"

Nodding, Marco climbed the stairs to the upper landing. The twins' room was softly lit with a small night-light and both girls were sound asleep in their beds.

He sagged against the door frame. Everything looked so normal. Everything was just how it'd been in Capri. Livia was curled up beneath the covers. Gia was curled up on top. Livia didn't move a lot in her sleep. Gia was a thrasher.

He felt ridiculously young, ridiculously vulnerable. He'd come to love the girls being here, loved having them back in his life. How could he lose them again? How could he let Payton come between him and his children again?

He couldn't, he silently answered. He wouldn't.

Blinking he pressed his forearm to his eyes. *Maledizione!* Why did this have to happen? Things had seemed to be working so well. Everything had felt right.

Biting back another oath, he carefully lifted Gia, pulled back the warm covers and slid her beneath the light down comforter. He drew the covers up to her shoulder.

As he adjusted the comforter, Gia stirred and opened her eyes. "Papa."

"*Ciao, mia bambina.*" He gently ran his hand across her forehead, smoothing the dark curls back from her high regal brow.

"Where's Mommy?"

A lump the size of a fist lodged in his throat. He fought the violence of his emotions. "Doing a few things."

"I miss her."

"She misses you, too."

"Is she coming to say good night?"

"Soon."

"Good." She smiled, content. "Kiss?"

Marco bent over, and gently kissed her.

Gia snuggled lower under the covers. "Tell Mommy to come soon."

Marco's eyes burned. How was this going to work? How would he keep the children from being terribly hurt?

He closed the door and stood in the hall for a long moment. What was he going to do? What should he do?

He was angry with Payton but he didn't hate her. He knew she'd been a good mother to the twins but she was so dishonest with him.

He heard the phone ring in a distant part of the house and it crossed his mind that it could be Payton. He hurried to his room to answer it.

"Marco." But it wasn't Payton. It was Marilena. How did she know he was back? How did she know that he wasn't on his honeymoon?

"It's late," he said shortly.

"Would you like to come over for a coffee?" The princess sounded so normal, so disarmingly casual.

"It's after midnight, Marilena."

"We've had coffee many times after midnight."

Not during my honeymoon. "It's been a long day."

"Then I can come there."

"Marilena—"

"She's here, Marco." The princess' voice suddenly dropped. "She's here and I don't know what to do."

"Payton?"

"Marco, she's very upset. She's not well, and I'm afraid—"

"She's not sick," he interrupted tersely, finding it humiliating having to even discuss it with Marilena. Damn Payton for going there. Damn Payton for dragging others into this—and Marilena of all people!

"I know," Marilena answered quietly. "I've known for a while." She drew a slow breath. "It's a long story, Marco. Will you come here, or should we go there?"

Payton wasn't with Marilena when Marco met the princess for coffee twenty minutes later. "She didn't come with you?" Marco asked, pulling his chair at the small city café that kept late hours.

"No. She left when I did, but she was on foot."

Marco's gut tightened. Payton shouldn't be walking alone this time of night. He didn't like the idea that she was out on her own. Women were vulnerable, especially in big cities. "Do you know where she was going?"

The princess shrugged. "She was upset. That's all I know."

They ordered coffees and while waiting Marilena lit up a cigarette. "I thought you gave up smoking years ago," Marco said, leaning against the table, elbows on the edge.

"I did. But I had to have one tonight." She drew on the cigarette. "So tell me, darling. Where should I begin?"

"The part where Payton tricks me into marriage again."

The princess slowly exhaled, blowing a small cloud of smoke. "Ah, a good place to start." She reached for espresso and took a small sip. "But the wrong place to start."

Marco felt the knot in his gut harden and double in size. He made a hoarse sound, something between a laugh and a snort. "Your point?"

"I couldn't do it after all." Marilena held the cigarette delicately, posture perfect. "I thought I could. I was sure I would. Jealousy isn't attractive, especially in women of a certain age, but I was jealous. Still am."

Marco was tempted to get up and walk out. He wasn't in the mood for this.

"The story is very simple, actually." She leaned forward to tap the ashes in the red aluminum ashtray. "I was at your house ten days ago when a doctor phoned from San Francisco. Payton was in the garden with the children. You were coming home for lunch but hadn't yet arrived."

Marilena's lips pursed. "I took the call. I said I was family and the doctor gave me the information. I thanked him nicely and promised to convey the news."

Ice water flooded his veins. "You knew."

"And I didn't tell." She drew on the cigarette

again, the tip glowing hot red. "It was my secret and it was my weapon—just in case I needed it."

And you did. "The lab report?"

She blew a small perfect smoke ring. "I phoned the doctor back and asked him to send a hard copy to me."

"You put the report under the door."

"I did." She suddenly crushed the cigarette and her lovely eyes filled with tears as she ruthlessly mashed the cigarette butt to nothing. "I loved you, Marco. More than I've ever loved anyone. Maybe that's why I can't keep my dirty deeds a secret."

Marco started to push away from the table. He'd wronged Payton. He'd absolutely humiliated her.

"The worst thing of all," Marilena said stopping him, "was when Payton came to my house today, she didn't blame me. She did not say one word against me. She simply asked for my help." The princess leaned back and shook her head. "She asked for *my* help."

CHAPTER THIRTEEN

MARCO returned to the villa. He could hardly see straight as he drove home. His vision blurred, his head throbbed. He felt as if he'd been slugged with one of the dressmaker's mannequins.

Payton hadn't known. Payton was totally in the dark.

He was such an ass. He was an arrogant fool. He wouldn't blame Payton if she couldn't forgive him.

He let himself into the house and flicked on the hall light. Pietra appeared and he nodded good night to her and the nanny quietly returned to her room.

Pietra would have told him if Payton returned. Marco's hands went to his hips and he gazed up the staircase. She wasn't up there. He knew she wasn't there. He would be able to feel it if she'd come home. But she hadn't come home and the house felt empty.

He tried to lie down but he couldn't sleep. He got up a couple hours later and went to the window in his bedroom. It was almost dawn. The street was silent. There was no traffic. The sky was beginning to lighten and soon the sun would rise.

If anything happened to her the girls would be devastated. Payton was the center of their world. They were like little planets and she was the sun around which they evolved.

It crossed his mind that the girls weren't the only ones that adored her. He did, too.

He thought of the future, realized that without the threat of cancer hanging over Payton's head, they could accomplish anything they wanted. Travel anywhere. Be anything. The sky was the limit.

She had to come home. He'd wait until morning and then if she didn't return, he'd go find her.

But in case she *did* come home, he wanted to be ready. He wanted desperately to apologize, to try again. Marco sat on the foot of the entry stairs with a champagne bottle and two crystal flutes. An hour passed. And then another. His eyes felt heavy. He nearly dozed off.

A key turned in the lock of the front door.

Payton walked into the house as if it were the most natural thing to do. She set down her suitcase, and then her purse. "Hello."

"Where have you been?" he asked, sitting forward.

She gestured behind her. "Sitting in a lot of cafés. Drinking too much coffee." She closed the front door. "What are you doing?"

"Waiting for you."

She looked at the champagne bottle sitting in melting ice water and the two empty flutes. "For a moment there I thought you were celebrating my departure."

"Never." He ran an unsteady hand through his hair. His eyes were gritty from lack of sleep. "I've been really worried. I came close to calling the police.

I was going to go looking for you if you didn't arrive soon."

Payton's lips quivered. Blue-tinged shadows shaded her eyes. "I don't know what to say, Marco."

"You don't have to say anything." He held out a hand to her, entreating. "Just come and sit here with me."

She looked at him for another long moment. She stared at his hand and then back up into his face. Her expression was infinitely sad. "I don't know that I can do that, either."

He nodded and dropped his arm, folding his hands between his knees. Marco stared at the faded golden carpet with the royal blue scrolls. The carpet had been here for over a hundred years. God knows the stories it could tell.

His eyes began to burn and blinking rapidly he tried to keep the carpet's faded pattern in focus. He was so relieved to have her home. He was so glad to know she was safe.

Best of all, he was very grateful to know that she wasn't sick and that she'd hopefully have many healthy years ahead of her. Years where she could hug the girls and chase them up stairs and wrestle them into bed.

Thank God she was okay.

Thank God she was home now, even if she didn't choose to stay.

Tears filled his eyes and he reached up to wipe away the tears with the pad of his thumb. "How did you get under my skin?" he choked, voice hoarse with emotions he could scarcely control. "How did you make me feel so much? Want so much?"

"The same way you made me feel so much. And love so much."

He hated crying, it was not a machismo thing. He'd never let anyone see him cry before. "I don't even know where to start with the apologies. I am so sorry. I am so sorry for losing my temper, behaving like an idiot, saying cruel things, walking out on you," he drew a breath. "For not listening to you, not trusting you—"

"I think I'm beginning to get the picture." Payton moved toward the stairs and slowly sat down on the bottom step, just one down from him. "What you're basically trying to say is that you're sorry for being a proud man who felt betrayed."

"But you didn't betray me."

Payton sighed and leaned against the stair railing. She gazed across the entry with the massive blue glass Venetian chandelier and the priceless oil paintings on the wall. One was of Pompeii with Mount Vesuvius erupting. The other was Naples two hundred years ago. "It's a strange start to a honeymoon, isn't it?"

He made a hoarse sound. "You want to call this a honeymoon?"

"I should think so. We're married and I'm not going anywhere."

Marco sat very still for a moment before he leaned forward. "Say that again."

She turned a little. Her elbow almost collided with Marco's shin. "I'm not going anywhere."

"You're staying?"

"Yes." And then she smiled crookedly. "We had a wedding, didn't we? I wore a dress this famous designer made, didn't I? And I live here, don't I?"

"Yes. Yes. And yes again." He caught Payton's face in his hands and covered her lips with his. *"Mia moglie,"* he whispered against her mouth. *My wife.*

"And don't you forget it!" Her heart was overwhelmed by everything that had happened and yet she refused to dwell on the sadness. Life was full of ups and downs. It had its glorious moments and its heartbreak, but in the end those who dream, and persevere, are rewarded.

"Tell me you forgive me," he said, stroking her cheek.

"I do."

"Thank God you didn't run away. Thank God you did come home."

Her eyes burned and filled with hot tears she couldn't let fall. "I thought about it. It was an attractive idea. I run off and you worry and suffer."

Her lips curved in a faint smile. "But then I realized this is the only place I want to be, and even if you were a complete barbarian today, you still deserved a second chance." She blinked and drew a huge breath. "So here I am."

"Thank God." His dark eyes shone. "Because I have some really good news for you."

She turned all the way around and leaned on his lap. "You do?"

"I do." He wrapped his arms around her and drew her closer so that she was cradled against his chest.

"A lab report came from your hospital in San Francisco. Payton, are you ready for this?"

The tears were filling her eyes and she didn't think she could hold them back this time. "No, what?"

"You don't have cancer!"

She didn't know whether to laugh or cry. "Really?"

"It was all a terrible mistake. You're perfectly, wonderfully healthy and I couldn't be happier. This is extraordinary. We must celebrate." He picked up the champagne bottle and the cork flew out with a loud pop.

The champagne bubbled and fizzed and Marco filled the two flutes. "To the best news I've ever heard. May you, my love, live a long, happy life."

They clinked glasses and drank. The champagne felt deliciously warm going down her throat and Payton savored the bubbles still lingering on her tongue before sitting up to kiss Marco. "And it will be a long happy life," she said, her heart beating fiercely, "if I spend it with you."

LIVE THE EMOTION

Modern Romance™
...seduction and
passion guaranteed

Tender Romance™
...love affairs that
last a lifetime

Medical Romance™
...medical drama
on the pulse

Historical Romance™
...rich, vivid and
passionate

Sensual Romance™
...sassy, sexy and
seductive

Blaze Romance™
...the temperature's
rising

27 new titles every month.

Live the emotion

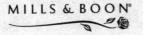

MILLS & BOON®

MB3

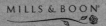

Margaret Way

Susan Fox

Jule McBride

With this Ring

An extra-special anthology
of three bridal short stories...

MILLS & BOON

Available from 18th April 2003

*Available at most branches of WH Smith,
Tesco, Martins, Borders, Eason, Sainsbury's
and all good paperback bookshops.*

0503/024/MB69

2 FREE

books and a surprise gift!

We would like to take this opportunity to thank you for reading this Mills & Boon® book by offering you the chance to take TWO more specially selected titles from the Modern Romance™ series absolutely FREE! We're also making this offer to introduce you to the benefits of the Reader Service™—

- ★ FREE home delivery
- ★ FREE gifts and competitions
- ★ FREE monthly Newsletter
- ★ Exclusive Reader Service discount
- ★ Books available before they're in the shops

Accepting these FREE books and gift places you under no obligation to buy, you may cancel at any time, even after receiving your free shipment. Simply complete your details below and return the entire page to the address below. *You don't even need a stamp!*

YES! Please send me 2 free Modern Romance books and a surprise gift. I understand that unless you hear from me, I will receive 4 superb new titles every month for just £2.60 each, postage and packing free. I am under no obligation to purchase any books and may cancel my subscription at any time. The free books and gift will be mine to keep in any case.

P3ZEA

Ms/Mrs/Miss/Mr ....Initials....................................

BLOCK CAPITALS PLEASE

Surname ....

Address ....

....

....Postcode..............................

Send this whole page to:
UK: FREEPOST CN81, Croydon, CR9 3WZ
EIRE: PO Box 4546, Kilcock, County Kildare (stamp required)